BLACK NANCY
BOOK III
THE
PRIVATEER

Lennox Nelson

To Michelle Miller
"Aw your journey"

Lennox

BOOK III: THE PRIVATEER

Also by Lennox Nelson
Black Nancy Book I
Black Nancy Book II: Ruby Rises

ISBN-13: 978-1519598448
ISBN-10: 1519598440

This book is dedicated to all our nameless ancestors lost at sea on the great passages.

BOOK III: THE PRIVATEER

CONTENTS

1   The Escape   1

2   The Ashanti Kraal   23

3   Not bad for a Mandinka   32

4   The Mortisi   38

5   Samburu's Return   44

6   The Road to Mt. Kilimanjaro   53

7   Future kings should not be on their knees   71

8   Training Day   77

9   First Mission   90

10   The Carolina Gold   102

11   The Bayou Belle   117

12   Mortisi Rise   125

13   A Student of History   136

14   Instrument of My Revenge   143

15   The Enemy of My Enemy   150

16   I Will Be Called Ramses   157

17   The Storm   162

18 Naira   175

19 Fight or Swim   182

20 Going to die on this night   209

21 Marooned   220

22 Birth of a Pirate   227

23 The Society   235

24 Everyday   250

25 Warrior Mother   257

26 A Decade has Passed   276

27 Letter of Marque   316

BOOK III: THE PRIVATEER

ACKNOWLEDGMENTS

Charming Son would like to thank all the bookstores, organizations and individuals that have supported our mission, to bring the Black Nancy Book Sagas to the masses: Bookbar (Denver, CO), Hastings Bookstore (Coeur d' Alene, ID), Ray and Jay of Revolution Books (Chicago, Il), Baltimore Inner Harbor Book Festival, Cynthia Stevenson and Syreeta Prince, Tyrone Sherrod and Living Classrooms of Baltimore, Maurice 'Picaso Moe' Morrison of MADD Graphics, for another phenomenal book cover and the editing duo of Stephanie Silva and Beverly Clavon Nelson. There are no words to adequately describe the gratitude I have for all your support! Thank you!

Lennox

Preface

Privateer is a term applied to a privately owned armed vessel whose owner or owners are commissioned by a hostile nation to carry on naval warfare. Such naval commissions or authorizations are called *Letters of Marque*. Privateering is distinguished from piracy, which is carried out without enlistment by a government. This book is based on true events.

CHAPTER 1

THE ESCAPE

Not far off the coast of West Africa, a Spanish Frigate, *Matador,* crashed through large waves as it tossed and rocked from side-to-side. The Bourbonic (Spanish National) Flag fluttered violently in the gusts of wind atop the main mast. Its crew scrambled about the deck, frantically pulling the ropes to lower the sails in a desperate attempt to keep from capsizing. Wooden pulleys squeaked as the sailors pulled in unison to finally bring the sails to rest at the bottom of the main mast where the wind could no longer catch them.

The massive iron anchor dropped into the sea

with a loud splash. The fancily dressed captain of the Spanish vessel looked around at the activity on his ship. He wore a large stylish blue hat with a long ostrich feather plume on the right side of it. He walked the deck with a smug look about him and his hands behind his back as he surveyed the crew's progress.

Once he reached the cargo hold, he bent at the waist and peered down into its darkness. Only the sound of chains clanking together could be heard in sync with the moans and groans of human cargo. The stench, unbearable in the heat of the African sun, was so repulsive that the Captain grabbed his lace handkerchief from inside his maroon, full length overcoat and covered his nose; trying desperately to mask the wretched odor of the hold from wafting into his nostrils. He turned to his first mate and shouted, "Traéme el Negro que conoce estas tierras!" ["Bring me up the Negro who knows these lands!"]

The first mate turned and quickly made his way to the ladder sticking out the top of the cargo hold. He climbed down into the hold and before the stench hit his nostrils, he heard the sound of a sickly, coughing, moaning female whimpering somewhere in the darkness.

Swarms of flies buzzed around the hold and around the first mate's head. He swatted at them with his left hand in front of his face before striking a wooden match on the wall beside him and lighting the torch that was hanging on the wall.

Once lit, he removed the torch from its holder and turned slowly, illuminating the entire hold, revealing the cargo of 50 Africans, male and female, chained side-by-side on their backs in rows of 25. Their movement was completely restricted by shackles on their ankles and necks, which were anchored to the hull of the ship by thick, linked chains. The captives had been in the hold for so long that the limited light of the torch hurt their eyes terribly. Those strong enough lifted their arms and turned their heads as much as possible away from the light of the torch. Many of them pleaded to be released in multiple African dialects as he stepped over them, indifferently.

The pungent stench of urine and feces was becoming unbearable for him, so he removed the scarf from around his neck and covered his mouth and nose with it as he continued searching the bodies strewn throughout the hold.

The first mate came upon the string of slaves of which he'd been searching. Stepping over them he made his way back to the wall and removed a ring of keys next to where he'd grabbed the torch to light his way. As he fumbled through the keys, he walked back over to the string of slaves and shined his torch over each slave in the row in order to find the one the captain had sent him to retrieve.

A male slave reached up begging and pleading to be released. Ignoring him uncaringly, the first mate held the torch over the second slave, a male as well, who also pleaded incoherently. He continued down the line illuminating the captives one by one lowering his torch on each individual as he passed until he came upon a pregnant female lying dead with her eyes and mouth open. He looked down at the woman's body with little emotion, lifted his head toward the cargo hold opening and yelled, "Dos hombres vengan abajo y saquen esta perra muerta de aqui!" ["Two men come down and get this dead bitch out of here!"] Two crewmen immediately scurried down the ladder to carry out the first mate's orders.

Finally finding the right key on the large ring, the first mate used it to unlock the shackles on the dead pregnant woman's ankles. The crewmen grabbed the woman by her feet and hands and lifted her from the urine soaked floor. They lumbered back to the ladder and began to ascend with the dead pregnant woman's body dangling lifelessly.

The first mate placed the torch over the next slave in the row. The slave he was seeking was a young male who lay motionless but aware. He was around 18 years of age with an athletic build, and handsome. His skin was the color of dark chocolate and he was much larger than the other male slaves restrained in the hold. The male slave looked up at the first mate, as if he had been expecting him. The young male slave had an eerie calm about him.

The first mate placed the key into the shackles on the ankles of the young captive then unlocked the larger shackle on his neck. After being released from his bonds the young male slave calmly sat up. After a few more moments, to get the feeling back into his lower extremities, he stood and attempted to balance himself on the floor of the rocking vessel.

The first mate grabbed the young male slave by the arm forcefully and moved him toward the ladder. He coerced him to climb the ladder toward the sunlight of the deck with a punch to the small of the boy's back. Not making a sound in pain or complaint, the young male slave began to climb the ladder with the first mate climbing closely behind him. Once on deck, the slave squinted from light sensitivity and covered his eyes.

The two crewmen who had removed the dead pregnant woman from the hold were standing at the bulwark of the ship. They playfully counted while swinging the dead woman's body back and forth to gain momentum to throw her body over the side of the ship and into the sea.

The young male slave listened as the two crewmen chuckled playfully as they counted.

"Uno! Dos! Tres!"

They released her lifeless body and it fell into the sea with a low, almost inaudible splash. The awaiting sharks immediately went into a feeding frenzy and attacked the body, ripping it apart with ease.

The first mate climbed out of the cargo hold just behind the young male slave and for no apparent reason kicked the young captive in the back. He fell to the deck and when he opened his eyes he was facing the fancy-French-shoe-wearing feet of the captain. The captain looked down at the boy as he questioned him smugly. "Donde estan tu gente? ["Where are your people?"]

The slave looked up at the Spanish captain quizzically and slowly rose to his feet, purposefully avoiding the captain's eyes. The captain, becoming impatient, pulled his sword with his left hand from its scabbard and carved a crude drawing of a hut into the wood of the ship's deck. After completing it he glared up at the young male slave and jabbed into the drawing with the tip of his sword. Becoming frustrated with the slave's inability to understand him the captain asked the same question he had before, but this time it was slower and much more deliberate, "Donde esta tu pueblo?"

["Where is your village?"]

Again, the young male slave looked at the Spanish captain confused. The captain not pleased with his inability to communicate with the young male slave glanced over at his first mate and quickly gestured with his head as he slowly placed his sword back into its scabbard.

Grabbing the young slave by the neck, the first mate lifted the boy to his feet and forced him toward the same bulwark the crewmen had earlier thrown the dead pregnant slave over. He forced the young slave to look over the rail at the sharks below feeding on the pregnant slave's body, which now only consisted of bloody chunks in the water.

The young male slave watched as the sharks swam through and chomped on whatever flesh remained of the woman's body in the small crimson pool of blood within the vast ocean. Opening their mouths wide, they showed every triangular shaped, razor-sharp tooth inside of their powerful jaws. The first mate shook the boy by the neck as he pointed down to the sharks. "Si no le dices al capitan lo que quiere saber, tu seras la siguiente comida!" ["You will be their next meal if you do not tell the captain what he wants to know!"]

The young male slave looked on horrified as tears began to roll down his cheeks. He turned and faced the first mate then, reluctantly, nodded his head.

The Spanish captain smiled smugly as he watched the young male slave nod to the first mate. Pulling the young male slave away from the bulwark, the first mate began walking the boy toward the captain with a proud look upon his face. Simultaneously, the captain walked toward them. The young male slave was forced once again to kneel in front of the captain.

While kneeling, the young male slave noticed a caltrop at the base of the main mast. He concentrated on it. He could hear his heart beating fast within his chest as he stared at the caltrop. With the agility of a cat the boy sprung to his feet from his knees and kicked the first mate in the groin with his right heel.

The first mate dropped to his own knees in anguish as he let go of the young male slave's neck and grabbed his groin with both hands. The young slave ran over to the caltrop and grabbed it. He spun around and ran toward the Spanish captain.

The captain attempted to draw his sword, but before his sword cleared its scabbard the young male slave dove on him and began jabbing the caltrop's spike into the side of the captain's neck repeatedly. Blood gushed from the neck of the captain with each impact of the boy's jabs.

The captain fell backward onto the deck with the slave on top of him striking him over and over again in a blind rage. The young male slave's attack was so fast that the members of the crew hadn't yet realized what was transpiring.

Once the captain's back hit the deck, the slave rolled over athletically and jumped to his feet in one motion. The two crewmen were so preoccupied with the sight of the shark frenzy feasting on the slave they'd just thrown overboard, that they were oblivious to what had just happened to their captain.

The first mate yelled to the crewmen and pointed to the young male slave sprinting towards them. The young male slave ran straight toward the two crewmen; his right hand, covered in the captain's blood and still holding the caltrop.

Desperate to get their attention, the first mate yelled and pointed again at the two crewmen. Both of them finally heard the first mate's cries but it was too late for them to react. The young male slave was barreling down on them and dove into them sideways. All three of the men plunged into the waters below!

Once in the water, the two crewmen try to swim away from the young male slave. One of them screamed in agony as the sharks attacked him mercilessly. He reached up to the ship in vain as he disappeared under the turquoise surf.

The remaining crewman attempted to swim away from the young male slave who pursued him. The young male slave, a much better swimmer than the crewman, caught up to him with ease. The crewman pleaded with the boy for his life. Staring at him emotionlessly, the young male slave raised his right hand out of the water and struck the crewman once with the caltrop in his left arm leaving a small puncture in it causing the crewman to bleed out into the shark infested waters. The young male slave looked into the eyes of the horrified crewman with all of the hate he possessed inside and just swam away toward the shore.

The crewman clutched his left arm with his right hand attempting to stop the bleeding. He treaded water and spun around frantically, waiting for the inevitable shark attack as the young male slave swam skillfully away. As the young male slave swam calmly to shore, he heard the last crewman scream in intense agony as the sharks ripped him apart. A small smile came over the young male slave's face as he continued toward shore.

Finally arriving at the shore, the young male warrior came out of the water breathing heavily after his long swim. He turned and saw the Spanish slave ship; he'd just escaped, anchored a few miles off shore. As he attempted to catch his breath, a sharp pain in his hand commanded his immediate attention. He winced, as he lifted his right hand to assess the problem. It was bleeding profusely. Slowly, he opened it, revealing that his hand had been punctured all the way through. *'The spikes on the caltrop had to be the culprit'*, he thought.

He balled his hand into a fist, wincing in intense pain as he did so. The young male looked in all three directions along the shoreline trying desperately to get his bearings. He again turned towards the sea and saw crewmen from the ship in a longboat rowing quickly towards the shore. He turned and ran as fast as he could into the jungle in front of him.

The young male moved through the unfamiliar jungle cautiously. The air was thick with moisture and filled with the sounds of many different species of birds calling. The monkeys screeched loud warnings to one another that there was a stranger in their part of the jungle while other creatures went on about their daily toil. It was a familiar and comforting concert to the young male, who was feeling a bit safer now that he had made it into the jungle.

Suddenly, the birds and all the other animals in the jungle went simultaneously silent. The young male took a few more cautious steps before he realized that the jungle surrounding him had gone pin-drop silent. He looked behind him, then above in the trees, then side to side. The young male stopped and peered into the dense jungle. It was dark and eerie, except for a few bands of the sun's rays that managed to penetrate the jungle's canopy. His stomach tightened when he heard something or someone making the leaves rustle, then stop. He spun to see what made the sound but saw nothing. He heard more rustling sounds behind him caused him to spin around quickly—but still nothing.

He began to move through the jungle again, but this time with more haste. The young male looked down while moving and found a fallen tree branch. He stopped and broke off a long limb from the branch. He began sharpening the tip of the limb into a point by scraping it frantically on a rock he found on the ground next to the fallen branch.

The first mate stood on the bow of the longboat. He squinted as he strained his eyes scanning the shoreline for any sign of the young male slave. He wore a scowl of resolve upon his face, for he was determined to find and kill the escaped male slave who had slain his captain and embarrassed him in front of his entire crew.

The crewmen behind him rowed the oars powerfully in unison until they were only a few feet from shore. They lifted their individual oars out of the water as the bottom of the boat grinded to a stop in the sand of the beach only a few feet away from where the young male slave had come out of the surf moments earlier.

The first mate, without hesitation, leapt from the boat first and immediately pulled his flintlock pistol from his belt. His kept his eyes trained on the sand for any sign of the young male slave. He snapped his head around to the four crewmen who were anchoring the longboat on the sand and ordered them anxiously.

"Rapido! Rapido!"

One of the crewmen, an African, turned quickly when he heard the first mate's order. He was very dark, lean and fierce looking. Reaching back into the longboat, he grabbed his spear and cutlass from the bottom of the boat. He placed the cutlass into his belt on the side of his hip and kept the spear in his right hand, then apprehensively trotted over to the first mate.

"Senor, esta es la tierra de los Ashanti. Si ellos nos encuentren aqui..." ["Sir, this is the land of the Ashanti. If they find us here..."]

The first mate interrupted him, furiously as he

poked his pistol into the bottom of the African crewman's neck.

"No me importa a quien chingados le pertenece esta tierra! Quiero al Negro bastardo que mato a mi capitan al anochecer. Entiendes?" ["I don't care whose fucking land this is! I want that black bastard who killed my captain by nightfall! Do you understand?"]

The African crewman nodded to the first mate nervously as the other three crewmen reached into the longboat to retrieve their flintlock muskets. They moved quickly towards where the first mate and the African crewman were standing.

The first mate lowered his pistol from the African crewman's neck slowly. He continued to peer menacingly into his eyes as he spoke slowly and deliberately.

"Cuando encuentre este hasta que llego alli. Tengo algo especial en mente para el!" ["When you find this bastard, keep him alive until I get there. I have something special in mind for him!"]

The African crewman nodded nervously to the first mate, then turned and began tracking the young male slave by searching for signs on the beach. He walked a short distance before discovering a fresh footprint in the sand. Bending at the knees, the tracker got low to the ground to take a closer look at the track. He looked up into the direction the footprint went into the jungle and smiled sinisterly. The African crewman stood, turned slightly and signaled the first mate with his hand that he had found the young escaped slave's trail.

The first mate turned to his other crewmen excited.

"Rapido! Date prisa!" ["Quick! Hurry up!"] They all started to head toward the jungle with haste.

The African crewman trotted into the jungle with his spear pointed in the same direction at the ready. He disappeared into the dense foliage ahead of the other crewmen. He trotted about a hundred yards into the jungle before finding the second sign that the young male slave had come that way, a small branch had been broken along the trail. Feeling that he was very close to catching up with the young male slave he picked up the pace of his tracking and began to run following the trail with his head fixed on the ground.

He came upon a gigantic tree that had fallen across the trail sometime ago, but was startled and confused when he discovered the young male slave standing atop the tree defiantly. He had a makeshift spear clutched tightly in his hands and was pointing it threateningly in the direction of the African crewman.

The young male slave spoke to him in his West African dialect.

"Why do you hunt and capture your own people for these filthy barbarians, like a dog?"

Though he understood the young male slave's words, the African crewman breathing heavily turned his head in the direction of the other crewmen following and yelled, "Lo tengo! El esta aqui!"["I have him! He is here!"]

The first mate heard the African crewman's voice and smiled. He and his men move faster towards the direction of the tracker's voice. The young male slave slowly began to descend the trunk of the large tree, keeping his eyes fixed on the African crewman.

"Do you remember the pregnant woman they

just discarded like a piece of rancid meat?" The young male slave emotionally questioned. The African crewman nodded nervously.

"Yes, I remember."

The young male slave jumped down onto the ground in front of the African crewman, unafraid. His face cannot hide his internal strife, pain, and rage. He grows progressively angrier.

"Her name was Amhara. She was a princess of the Mandinka. She... she... was carrying my brother inside her!" Tears of rage began to stream down the face of the young male slave who was beside himself with anger.

The African crewman pondered what the young male slave was telling him. His spear started to shake in his hand as he became more afraid. "You mean the pregnant woman was your...?"

Without warning, the young male slave charged the African crewman. He swatted the crewman's spear away like a skilled warrior with his makeshift spear, and rammed it into the African's abdomen and straight through his back. Enraged, he lifted the crewman off of the ground with his spear and ran with him through the jungle only coming to a stop when they hit a large tree.

Muscles bulged in his arms and chest as the young male slave held the impaled African on the tree and yelled at him with such force that hundreds of birds flew from their nests in the canopy. "SHE...WAS...MY...MOTHER!"

He cried while blood spilled from the African Crewman's mouth and trickled down the shaft of the young male slave's spear. The African still clutching his own spear dropped it as his last breathe squealed from his lungs. He died while impaled in the tree.

At that moment, the first mate and the other crewmen ran into the clearing behind the young male slave. Speaking English in a thick Spanish accent he called out to the boy tauntingly.

"Hola, you black bastard! You have been much more trouble than your miserable hide is worth!"

Simultaneously, he and his men aimed their muskets and pistols at the young male slave.

The slave yanked his spear from the abdomen of the impaled African and his body fell back to the ground with a thud. He turned defiantly towards the crewmen. Pointing his spear in the direction of their position then began to walk slowly towards them.

His pistol trained on the young male slave, the first mate yelled to him.

"Detente! Detente! ["Stop! Stop!"]

Turning his head slightly to his crewmen he yelled, "Disparenle a este perro, a mi mando! ["Fire on this dog, on my command!"]

The first mate closed his left eye and aimed directly for the slave's chest. Suddenly, the sound of multiple arrows cutting through the air rivaled the jungle sounds.

The first mate and all of his men were hit by multiple black arrows in their faces and bodies and fell to the ground helpless.

The young male slave never broke stride as the arrows rained down on the first mate and his crewmen. He walked stoically over to where the first mate had fallen and watched him gasping for air, like a fish out of water. He coughed, as he choked on his own blood. The young male looked down at the first mate emotionless as he knelt down next to him and whispered in his right ear. At the same time the first mate could see multiple pairs of muscular African legs walk up behind the slave.

"These are my new friends, the Ashanti! This is *their* land. You and everyone like you are not welcome here!" He spat out angrily.

He stood as the first mate looked on in horror while he and the Ashanti warriors formed a circle around him with their bows on their backs and spears in their hands. In unison, the Ashanti warriors and the young male slave lifted the spears in their hands and stabbed him repeatedly. The first mate felt every puncture into his body as his life slowly faded away.

CHAPTER 2

THE ASHANTI KRAAL

The Ashanti hunting party trotted in a single file line out of the jungle into a vast and lush valley. Colorful birds streaked across the sky in huge flocks.

The young male slave trotted with them in the center of their formation, clutching his wounded hand. A few of the Ashanti warriors carried the flintlock muskets and cutlasses they had taken off the dead Spanish crewmen.

Once in the clearing, the young male warrior looked down from atop the huge hill just above what the Ashanti's called a kraal. They made their way down a skinny trail on the face of the hill, running through a huge herd of goats that scattered across the clearing before reaching their destination; the tall, thick wooden gates of the Ashanti kraal. The kraal was situated in a large man-made clearing next to a wide, rapid moving, buttermilk colored river.

Huge Ashanti warriors stood guard on top of the tall walls of the kraal. Each of them held a zebra hide shield, about the length of a man, in their left hands and an iron tipped spear in their right. All of them looked menacing. The huge gates of the kraal were opened just as the first warrior in line reached them.

The young male warrior marveled at the size of the gates and wall that surrounded the kraal as they trotted through the gate. More huge guards protected the front gate and stared stone-faced at the young male warrior as he entered the kraal.

In the distance he could hear the chronicler's voice announcing the return of the hunting party in Ashanti dialect. *"The hunting party has returned! The hunting party has returned! They bring with them an outsider!"* He shouted.

Dozens of Ashanti began to pour out of their small huts to catch a glimpse of the outsider. The young male warrior grew uncomfortable as villagers started to line the pathway that he and the hunting party were walking through. Most of them stared at him suspiciously. He could feel their contemptuous gaze upon him.

Atop of his large throne, the chief of the

Ashanti sat in the very center of the kraal. His massive throne was covered in lush lion and cheetah fur. Huge elephant tusks towered and curved towards each other slightly in the rear of his throne making a semi-circle behind him. The chief was a large and muscular man with very dark skin. His hair and beard were gray. He wore a cheetah fur robe with a matching crown.

The young male warrior looked up at the chief's throne in awe as he and the Ashanti hunting party neared the chief.

Suddenly, a beautiful, young, adolescent woman appeared from behind the chief's throne and stood by his side. Her hair was very short and her body was chiseled and powerful like an athlete.

The young male warrior noticed that her robes were also made from cheetah fur, which she wore off her shoulders. She also donned a smaller version of the same crown as the chief. He could see the handles of her Tutsi sickle knives to either side of her head. Her breasts and womanhood were covered with a white leopard skin loincloth and top. He thought to himself that he had never seen a woman warrior so beautiful.

The people of the village started to fill the circle in the center of the kraal. A loud murmur filled the air as the hunting party and the young male warrior reached the circle. The villagers moved out of the way of the hunting party as it approached.

Once near the throne, each member of the hunting party walked in front of the chief and knelt, then bowed their heads to him in homage.

The young male warrior stood defiantly as he stared at the young woman beside the chief. Smirking, the young woman noticed that the young warrior was gazing at her. Bashfully, she shot him a quick smile then tried to look more serious before anyone noticed.

The crowd's indistinguishable chatter grew louder until the chief stood, then all murmuring ceased. He pointed regally.

"Who is this outsider and why have you brought him to my kraal?" He thundered.

A tall and lanky member of the hunting party looked up at the chief nervously and spoke, "My chief, this boy escaped from the Spaniard's ship anchored off our shores; the one you sent us to investigate! Oh Mighty One, it was a slave ship!"

The villagers cringed and began to murmur once more until the chief raised his hands and the murmuring stopped once more.

Unimpressed, the chief rebutted. "My question remains unanswered. Why have you brought him to *my* kraal? Do the Ashanti pick up strays in the jungle?" He laughed hardily. The villagers followed suit and laughed as well.

The hunting party leader looked around at the villagers laughing. He dropped his head and scowled. After taking a quick, deep breath he lifted his head once more to the chief.

"No sire. We do not. But, this boy has proven himself a fine warrior! He killed the captain of the ship, and two... no three of the crew who chased him onto our shores!" The leader explained apologetically.

The chief thought for a moment, then, nodded his head in approval. Staring down at the young male warrior he questioned, "Is this true, boy? Did you end the lives of all these men?"

The young warrior glared up at the chief confidently.

"Yes, I killed all those men, and I plan to kill

a lot more of them! I mean, that is if your majesty would do me the honor of not taking my life!"

The crowd chuckled collectively at the boy's coy response.

Chuckling as well, the chief turned his head slightly to the right and glanced at the young woman. The young woman nodded to the chief. The chief turned his head back toward the young warrior. "What is your name boy and which tribe claims you?"

Staring directly at the young woman, the young warrior responded proudly. "My name is Bambara! Son of Umemeh and Amhara! I am the eldest son of house Umemeh and heir to the throne and future king of the Mandinka people!"

The crowd let out a collective gasp in surprise. A murmur of indistinguishable communication rose from the villagers again. The woman at the side of the chief smiled slyly at Bambara.

Bambara bowed his head slightly to the young woman, keeping his eyes trained on her as he did so flirtatiously. The chief sat back on his throne rubbing his chin as he pondered for a moment. He looked down at Bambara.

"Prince Bambara, if you were I... what would you do with you?"

He lifted his wounded hand. Blood leaked down his right arm onto the ground before he addressed the chief.

"First, great chief! I would allow me to tend to my wounded hand! Then, I would allow me to train with twenty of your warriors. Let me make myself clear, I am only interested in warriors brave enough to volunteer to train and fight alongside me! I would then allow these twenty warriors and myself to rain down the wrath of the Gods upon the heads of the barbarian invaders who continue to rip our people from this land, to take them off to distant shores and enslave them.

Lastly, I would allow me to destroy any of the tribes who have assisted the barbarians in any way! As a symbol of my loyalty to you, great chief and the Ashanti people, I will follow the customs and laws of the Ashanti people. From this day forth, Bambara, Prince of the Mandinka shall be known as Bambara, warrior of the Ashanti!"

The Ashanti villagers erupted into a deafening cheer, as they pumped their fists into the air. They began to dance with one another, as African drums played a fast, rhythmic beat.

The chief turned and looked at the young woman beside him. He was impressed. He leaned over to her and whispered.

"Oh, I like this one."

He then turned, smiled and stood.

"I, Chief Yoruba of the Ashanti, decree that Bambara of the Mandinka will be allowed to become one of us, if he so chooses!"

The villagers went wild with the news and started to dance more animatedly.

Bambara stepped forward and knelt at the feet of Chief Yoruba. He turned his head slightly to the left to catch a closer glimpse of the young woman. The young woman glared back at Bambara unafraid as the people celebrated around them. She left the side of Chief Yoruba and walked toward Bambara confidently.

Bambara stood and concentrated on each of the young woman's steps in his direction. He studied her every move no matter how subtle.

Once she arrived where Bambara was

standing, the young woman reached out and lifted his wounded hand gently. "We must take care of this hand, so that you can kill many more of our enemies with it," she said in a sultry but menacing manner.

Bambara smiled widely at the young woman. He knew instinctively from her mannerisms that she was no ordinary woman.

"What is your name, my warrior princess?"

The young woman lifted her head from his hand and looked into Bambara's eyes.

"I am called Fulani."

"I will never forget that name." Bambara proclaimed.

Fulani smiled and blushed.

"Come with me, I will take you to our healer."

Bambara and Fulani made their way through the joyous crowd together. The villagers made way for them to pass as they looked on at the both of them in awe.

Chief Yoruba watched as the two of them walked through the crowd hand in hand. He giggled and nodded his head approvingly.

CHAPTER 3

NOT BAD FOR A MANDINKA

Bambara walked out of his hut early enough to see the sun rising over the distant mountains in the east. His hut was situated on the banks of a wide river, nestled between two trees which provided much needed shade on his home when the sun was at its highest. Bambara took in a deep breath as he studied and admired his view of the valley surrounding him.

A herd of hippos kept cool and played across the river. He watched as they submerged themselves into the murky river water only to ascend once more many feet from where they had started chomping on fish they'd caught while underwater.

Bambara looked overhead and watched the aerial acrobatics of a mother hawk teaching her three chicks how to stalk prey.

He looked down at his wounded hand, which

was wrapped tightly with a piece of Kente cloth. Bambara began to unwrap the cloth to take a closer look at his hand. Once unwrapped, he studied the circular scar left from the puncture wound through his hand. The wound had almost totally healed. He opened and closed his hand in attempt to loosen the muscles and tendons inside of it. He walked over to a table in the center of the training area that had been built for him. The area had all of the vegetation removed from the ground, so all that remained was a flat, dirt-filled ring.

Obstacles had been set up all throughout the ring. Large, oval-shaped targets made from straw, lined one area. Spears, bows and arrows were on stands in another. Another area housed several straw men that had been fashioned to look like an enemy running. The last area had a high wall with ropes for climbing and was situated at the end of the demanding obstacle course.

Bambara took a deep breath with his eyes closed to center himself. He opened them again and sprinted over to the area with the targets in a line. He grabbed a spear and threw it towards the first target. The spear cut through the air and hit the target dead center for a bull's-eye. Again, he grabbed another spear and hurled it towards the second target. It also cut through the air and hit its mark, striking the target very close to the center. Bambara ran to the next area where the straw enemies were running. Effortlessly, he grabbed a bow and skillfully placed an arrow into it, took aim and fired.

The arrow pierced the neck area of a straw-man target. Quickly, he reached for another arrow, took aim and prepared to loose it.

Fulani, watching Bambara prepare to fire, interrupted. "Not bad for a Mandinka!" She yelled sarcastically.

Bambara was startled and let the arrow fly inadvertently. The arrow missed everything, flew into the jungle, and harmlessly landed into some bushes. He looked over at Fulani displeased.

Fulani smiled and walked towards Bambara chuckling. "It is not hard to hit a target that is not moving or trying to kill you back," she mocked.

Bambara smiled as he removed another arrow. "If the princess thinks she can do better, she is more than welcome to try!" he said sarcastically as he lifted the bow and arrow in Fulani's direction and bowed his head.

She took the bow and arrow from him awkwardly as if it was her first time holding one.

Bambara smirked doubtfully as he instructed Fulani.

"All right, now Princess, select your target."

The princess appeared to be having trouble even pulling the arrow back in the bow. The target she selected was one of the running straw-men targets.

Bambara continued to instruct her.

"Now, take a deep breath before loosing the arrow." He turned his head toward the target before Fulani let the arrow fly. She took an overly exaggerated deep breath.

Bambara giggled to himself, as he had anticipated her firing the arrow.

She prepared to fire but at the last moment she removed the tension from the bow and brought the arrow back to resting position. Fulani turned toward Bambara.

"Are you sure this is the proper way to shoot, Mandinka?"

Bambara struggled to suppress his laughter. "Yes, Princess. I am sure."

Fulani snapped her head back into the direction of the target and pulled the arrow all the way back until the wood of the bow creaked under the strain. She closed her left eye slowly and breathed steady before letting the arrow fly. The arrow struck the straw man target in the center of its face. Quickly, she grabbed another arrow and fired without any pause and hit the same target in the chest. Fulani again grabbed another arrow and fired it rapidly, hitting the same straw target in the area his penis would be. A large bird squawked over their heads. The princess loaded the bow once more. She took aim on the bird hovering above and concentrated on its effortless movement as it hovered on the warm updrafts from the river. Suddenly, she loosed the arrow. The bird squawked one last time before falling from the sky and into the dirt of the training area.

Bambara stood dumbfounded as the bird hit the ground. He turned toward Fulani, speechless. Fulani smiled smugly as she tossed the bow back to Bambara. He caught the bow and stood perplexed as Fulani strolled by.

Fulani walked by Bambara, then stopped, turned and stepped to him until there was only about a foot of distance between them.

"Uh, I almost forgot. Consider me your first volunteer. When shall I return for my instruction?" she asked coyly.

Bambara, still reeling from Fulani's awesome display of archery, stood there in disbelief. He stammered when he answered the princess' query.

"Well... uh... t, tomorrow. Yes, tomorrow. At, uh... At, uh... sunrise."

Fulani turned and walked away. She intentionally exaggerated her hip-sway, teasing Bambara with a smile on her face.

"See you at sunrise, Mandinka?" she yelled as she disappeared over the hill.

Bambara looked down at the bow, shook his head, and giggled impressed with the display he had just witnessed.

CHAPTER 4

THE MORTISI

The next morning a heavy mist blanketed the valley. Bambara stepped out of his hut rubbing his eyes after a very good night's slumber.

Naked, he made his way slowly to the river's edge. He cupped his hands and lifted the cool water from the river and splashed it into his face to wake himself. Next, he placed water into his mouth and swirled it around inside a few times before spitting it out. He picked up a small twig and began to scrape each tooth. He stopped scraping for a moment because he felt as if he was being watched. Bambara stood and pivoted quickly with his penis dangling.

Much to his surprise, Fulani was standing in front of the training circle smirking as she stared directly at his manhood. Holding a spear in her right hand with the blunt end of it on the ground, she wore a revealing harness made of leather. It crossed in front of her body, barely covering her breasts from either side. The handles of her Tutsi sickle knives he could be seen from both sides of her head.

Bambara, embarrassingly startled, attempted to cover his penis with both hands.

"Apparently, when a Mandinka tells you sunrise, he means a different time of day!" Fulani scoffed playfully.

Bambara awkwardly moved toward his hut still clutching his privates as he went inside. A few seconds later, he returned outside tying his loincloth as he walked toward Fulani.

"No, Princess, I meant now. I expected more of your warriors to heed my call though. Not to sound too disappointed at the prospect of just training with you, but two warriors does not make much of a war party."

Fulani looked at Bambara slyly.

"You are correct, Bambara. That is why I brought you a few more volunteers."

She moved the spear to her armpit and clapped her hands twice, loudly. Suddenly, out of the mist, the sound of many spears being slapped against animal hide shields could be heard. The mist lifted slightly and revealed nineteen fearsome Ashanti warriors lined up side by side across the center of the training area.

Bambara was beside himself with excitement. He quickly walked toward the warriors and inspected them as he made his way down their line. He recognized the warrior in the center. It was the leader of the hunting party. Bambara stopped and stepped closer to the warrior. "Welcome, my friend. I am glad to see you have decided to join me. What are you called?"

The warrior stepped forward in military fashion. Shouting for all to hear.

"I am called Adangbe. My men and me have come to fight with you! Die for you or die with you! To this we swear to the gods!" Adangbe knelt in front of Bambara. The other warriors dropped to their knees as well.

"We swear to the gods!"

Bambara was taken aback by the warrior's decree. He turned his head toward Fulani, who was smiling. She bowed her head slightly to Bambara. He gave her an approving glance and then snapped his head back to his warriors with a determined look.

"Stand, my brothers!"

The warriors quickly stood in unison.

"It does my heart good to see that there are still men in this land who are not afraid to do what must be done to rid ourselves of the foreign slave traders and their accomplices here. I have lost my mother and unborn brother to this disease. I know many of you, if not all, have lost or know someone who has lost someone to this evil!"

Fulani walked up to the left side of Bambara and stood proudly.

"But, hear me now! I am no longer Mandinka! You... are no longer Ashanti! We are all Mortisi now! In Mandinka it means 'Bringers of Death'. When our enemies look upon us they will know that they will never see their homes or loved ones again! To this I swear in blood!"

Bambara turned to Fulani and slid his right hand down the tip of the spear she was holding. He turned his bloody hand towards the warriors.

Fulani, Adangbe and the other warriors cut their hands on their spears as well and held them up for each other to see.

Adangbe turned and faced the other warriors. He began to chant slow and ominously.

"Mortisi! Mortisi! Mortisi!"

The other warriors began to chime in. They moved closer to Adangbe forming a tight circle and banging the butts of their spears into the ground chanting in unison,

"Mortisi! Mortisi! Mortisi!"

Bambara and Fulani looked at one another proudly. They too began to chant with the warriors and moved into the circle with the others.

Suddenly, drumming erupted from the center of the kraal. The Mortisi stopped chanting and listened to the message the distinct drumbeat signified.

Bambara looked around at the warriors, confused. As the drums reverberated through the valley, Fulani's face lit up with unbridled excitement.

"It's Samburu! Yes, Samburu has returned to us!"

Bambara turned to Fulani still confused. *"Samburu? Who was this Samburu, and why was he so important to Fulani?"* He thought as he became slightly jealous at her excitement to see whoever he was. Before he could ask who this man was, Fulani took off running back toward the main gate of the kraal yelling ecstatically.

"My brother! My brother has returned!"

Hearing her boisterous declaration, Bambara's jealousy subsided. Adangbe approached Bambara to fill him in on just who Samburu was.

"Bambara, Prince Samburu has been away negotiating trade agreements with the tribes of the south. We must go into the kraal to receive him, or I assure you he will want to know the reason why we did not." He cautioned.

Bambara waved his arm in the direction of the kraal. He and the Mortisi trotted toward the kraal where the drums began to beat stronger and more rapid.

CHAPTER 5

SAMBURU'S RETURN

The Ashanti villagers danced and waved colorful oversized umbrellas made of fine material and adorned with golden heads of various animals, such as lions, tigers, giraffes, and eagles. Many of the male villagers wore colorful traditional headdresses, while gyrating and swinging their arms wildly during the ancient celebratory dance in the very center of the kraal. Drummers played feverishly as the villagers danced around them cheering and singing merrily.

Chief Yoruba regally strolled out of his large hut followed by a small contingent of wives and advisers. He smiled widely as he raised his arms in acknowledgement of the people's celebration.

Samburu entered the kraal atop a slow, lumbering camel. He was stoically handsome, thin and dark with very smooth skin. His clothing was distinctively European, which consisted of a safari hat, a frilly white long sleeved shirt, riding pants and knee-high black leather riding boots. Samburu smiled graciously and nodded to the Ashanti villagers who lined the way through the kraal. Periodically, he bent over and shook the hands of some of them. He waved to them as well, like a conquering hero. Following him were twenty fierce looking Ashanti bodyguards walking in columns of two.

Behind them followed many commoners who were leading another caravan of camels that carried large wooden barrels and crates on their backs.

Samburu rode his camel to the center of the kraal where Chief Yoruba was seated on his throne. He tapped the camel on its head with his riding stick. The camel let out a loud bellow then bent its front legs and lowered its head close to the ground. Still acknowledging the crowd as he hopped off the camels back, Samburu turned and walked quickly toward Chief Yoruba.

The chief awaited his son eagerly on his throne, until he could not contain himself any longer and jumped to his feet to greet him. The two of them embraced lovingly. Chief Yoruba looked into the sky. "My son has returned to me safely!"

"I thank you, Nyame for this blessing!" The chief lowered his head and looked into the eyes of Samburu.

"I have missed you, my son."

Samburu smiled at his father.

"I have missed you as well, father. I have much to share and discuss with you."

Both of them turned together and walked toward the throne, then in unison turned and faced the villagers who were still celebrating. Chief Yoruba raised his hands and all dancing and cheering ceased. The kraal fell dead silent. The chief raised Samburu's left hand with his right.

"Tonight we shall feast in honor of the safe return of your future Chief, my son Prince Samburu!"

He proclaimed proudly then laughed hardily as he released Samburu's hand. The chief returned to his throne and sat. The villagers let out a deafening cheer and the drumming, dancing and merriment whipped up again. Samburu surveyed the people dancing. He turned his head slightly to Chief Yoruba.

"Father, where is the sprout, where is...?

At that very instant Fulani ran through the throngs of people and sprinted up to where Samburu was standing next to the throne. She jumped into his arms like a little girl.

Samburu swung her around in a circle as they hugged each other tightly. Excitedly, Fulani addressed her brother.

"Oh, how I've missed you, brother!"

Samburu released Fulani and pushed her away gently to arm's-length smiling widely.

"Let me look at you!"

He looked her up and down as he smirked and nodded his head. Fulani playfully spun around like a model for Samburu.

"My, how beautiful you have become, sister. Have you had any worthy suitors I should know about in my absence?"

Chief Yoruba scoffed instantly at Samburu's question.

"Ha! She won't give anyone the time of day, son. All she cares about is fighting and practicing fighting and training and war!" he sighed exaggeratedly.

"I've all but given up on the prospect of having a grandchild from this one before my time has passed!"

Fulani rolled her eyes at her father and returned her gaze upon her brother and grinned.

"I've gotten very skilled with my sickle knives, brother. Watch! I'll show you!"

Fulani snatched the two Tutsi sickle knives from behind her head and skillfully began to twirl them in front of her body then behind. The sickle knives could be heard cutting through the wind as she demonstrated.

Samburu watched and admired his sister's skillful exhibition for a few seconds then interrupted impatiently.

"Perhaps you can show me your skill as a warrior another time, sister."

Frustrated, Chief Yoruba chimed in.

"Do you see? What did I tell you? What man of noble birth wants a wife that can defeat him in battle? I'll tell you... None!" He sighed.

Bambara and his Mortisi warriors trotted in front of Chief Yoruba, Fulani, and Samburu. They all knelt before the royal family with their heads down.

Fulani twirled her sickle knives once more then skillfully returned them to the holders behind her head. She turned and smiled at Bambara.

Samburu noticed how his sister was gazing at Bambara affectionately. Bambara stood and bowed his head toward Samburu respectfully and placed his right hand over his heart.

"Greetings to you, Prince Samburu! Please, allow me to..."

The prince interrupted Bambara rudely and pointed at him in anger before addressing him in a condescending tone.

"Who is this, speaking to, and greeting me, as if he and I have known each other for years?"

Fulani ran to Samburu and stood beside him smiling.

"Brother, this is..."

Samburu cut Fulani off mid-sentence.

"Silence! I asked this dog who he was... not you, sister!"

Fulani flinched toward Samburu but controlled herself and returned, frowning, to her father's side.

Instantly, Samburu's bodyguards ran toward Bambara and the villagers stopped their celebration to move out of the way of the princes' men simultaneously.

The Mortisi stood in unison, turned and locked their shields forming a wall, while simultaneously snapping their spears in the direction of the converging bodyguards.

Bambara took an aggressive posture as he glared up at Samburu and rebutted cool and defiant.

"If my prince thinks he sees a dog, why does he not come down here and attempt to train it."

Samburu scoffed at the affront of Bambara and quickly started to descend towards him.

"I am still the ruler of the Ashanti, am I not? Chief Yoruba pointed, "This man is Bambara, a prince of the Mandinka and our guest! So, you and your men will act accordingly! Do I make myself clear?" he declared in a most ominous and deep voice.

Samburu (chest swollen with aggression) stopped and glared ominously at Bambara. Bambara glared back at Samburu, at the ready.

Waving his hand, Samburu signaled his men to stand down. His bodyguards instantly put their spears at rest and returned to the caravan. Samburu then turned to his father and bowed his head showing his fealty.

"Of course, father. Forgive me; I have been away for too long. My manners escape me. Please accept my humblest apologies!"

Chief Yoruba grinned proudly at Samburu and stood. He raised his arms once more.

"No harm done my son. We need more dancing, more drumming! I cannot wait to see the wonders you have brought back for me to peruse. I would like for you to dine with your father tonight, no excuses! And do not wear those barbarian rags either. When you feast with me it will be as the Prince of the Ashanti!"

Chief Yoruba walked up to Samburu and placed his right arm around the back of his son's neck as they strolled together toward the caravan. Drumming started again and the people began to celebrate in the kraal once more.

Bambara and Samburu exchanged one last contemptuous glance as Samburu and Chief Yoruba walked down from the throne. The chief stopped momentarily and turned his head toward Bambara.

"Bambara, you will also dine with us tonight. Do not be late!"

"It would be an honor, Oh, Great One," replied Bambara.

He bowed his head respectfully to Chief Yoruba then glanced up at Fulani before turning to leave the kraal with the Mortisi following closely behind.

Fulani, frustrated, turned and walked into the large hut behind the throne.

CHAPTER 6

THE ROAD TO MT. KILIMANJARO

Chief Yoruba laughed hardily as he looked down the barrel of a flintlock musket with his left eye closed. He peered through the aiming sight with his right. The chief pointed the barrel to the ground before pulling the trigger. The hammer moved forward and clicked. Laughing, he grabbed the large wooden goblet sitting in front of him on the corner of the massive rectangular dining table, filled with an alcoholic beverage. He took a long gulp from the goblet then passed the musket to a slender, dark brown servant girl, who awkwardly grabbed the weapon with both hands and walked it over to where Samburu was seated at the other side of the table. She bowed, handed the musket to Samburu respectfully before leaving the chief's hut. Samburu raised his goblet to Chief Yoruba.

"To you, father... and to the Ashanti Empire!"

He took a long drink from the goblet before

placing it back onto the table with a wide grin. Samburu studied the flintlock musket in his hands.

"Well, what do you think, father? I've made quite a few connections in my travels. The kind of connections that give me... excuse me, I mean you, access to hundreds of these new weapons. Just think of it, father..." Samburu clutched his fist tightly has if he were crushing a bug, then continued. "With these weapons... the power you could wield!"

Chief Yoruba held his empty goblet up in his right hand. Quickly, another servant girl rushed over and filled his cup with more libations. He looked uninterested in what Samburu was trying to discuss.

"My son, I will never use these European fire sticks. Besides, I already wield all the power that one man could ever hope to. What more could I want?"

Chief Yoruba switched his filled goblet into his left hand and palmed the buttocks of the young servant girl. He laughed loudly and took another long swig from his cup.

Samburu, disappointed to hear his father's

position, attempted unsuccessfully to conceal his displeasure.

"But why, father? When will you see that these weapons are the future of warfare?"

Chief Yoruba continued to sip nonchalantly from his goblet. He gazed across the table at his son.

"These weapons, like the men who created them, have no soul."

The chief stood and walked to the guard at the entrance of his hut. He took another sip before snatching the guard's spear away with his opposite hand. He drank the remainder of the contents from his goblet and threw it to the ground. Samburu watched his father in contempt, but forced himself to smile.

Skillfully, Chief Yoruba twirled the spear around in his hands, then around his waist and finally, around his neck with little effort as he spoke again.

"It is not the weapon itself, because if I were to lay this spear on the ground, it would just lay there. But, when a man takes the time, to practice and master his weapon, well then... it becomes lethal! Our weapons force you to become one with them and that is when its true power can be harnessed and unleashed!"

The chief twirled the spear back into his hands and stopped. Suddenly, he threw the spear over the head of Samburu, hitting the lion's head that was mounted on the wall between the eyes.

Fulani clapped, as she stood in the entrance of her father's dwelling.

"Well done father! I see that I am not the only one in this family who practices the art of war!"

Chief Yoruba bowed toward Fulani playfully. "Thank you, daughter. Did I ever tell you of the time I was surrounded by 20... no, 30 Zulu warriors?"

Fulani walked into the hut and took a seat at the table next to her father's chair. She rolled her eyes up in her head and sighed deeply.

"Yes, father, you've only told us this story a hundred times and each time the number of Zulus grows!" She scoffed then smiled sweetly at him. The chief walked to his chair and sat. He reached for and took Fulani by the hand and smiled at her.

Samburu looked on.

"Hello, sister! You look radiant tonight as usual."

She turned her head towards Samburu and nodded confidently.

"Thank you, brother. So, what were you and father in the midst of discussing?"

Samburu chuckled. "Fulani, you must help me with him. Father and I were discussing how we as a people must change with the times or find ourselves trampled by them."

Fulani reached for a bowl of grapes on the table. She picked one off the bunch and popped it into her mouth, pondering as she chewed.

"Why must we change brother? We Ashanti have ruled this land for thousands of years. Our civilization is millennia older than your friends, the Europeans. We welcomed them here with open arms and how did they repay our kindness, brother? I'll tell you how, with bondage, treachery, illness and slavery! They sail here from all over to steal our most precious resource, our people! I'm sorry, brother, but I agree with father. The only way to protect our people is to rid them of all of these colorless barbarians!"

Chief Yoruba applauded and banged on the

table with his left hand, as he laughed.

Samburu glared at Fulani and shook his head. He composed himself and then raised his goblet to her. "I've been gone too long. I forgot that you and father are of the same mind on most things. I must concede defeat on this topic." *For now*, he thought to himself.

He drank from his goblet then slammed it down on the table and turned his head toward Fulani. Slyly he continued.

"Now, onto a far more intriguing topic. Father, when did we start allowing Mandinkas to join our ranks? That insolent boy today-- where did he come from? And why was he at the head of some of our finest warriors?"

"Because unlike you, my prince, I will never take on the mantle of friend to those who would enslave me!" Bambara interrupted, as he stood stoically in the threshold of the chief's hut.

Samburu insulted, stood quickly.

"I have allowed you to live only because of my father... but don't tempt me, boy!"

Fulani smirked at Chief Yoruba, who grinned as well.

Bambara bowed toward the chief and Fulani.

"I am sorry, Chief Yoruba. I mean no disrespect but maybe it would be better if I did not dine with you tonight."

Samburu stayed seated but kept his eyes locked on Bambara. Chief Yoruba stood and reached out with his left hand smiling.

"Nonsense, you young men are just having a spirited debate. I'm rather enjoying all of this vim and vigor. If you ask me, there's not enough of that around here. Isn't that right, Fulani?"

She turned and smiled flirtatiously at Bambara.

"Yes, father, you're right. There isn't enough passion around here lately."

Fulani cut a mischievous glance at Samburu.

Bambara nodded toward Chief Yoruba and walked over to the table and sat on the opposite side facing Fulani. They looked at one another and smiled shyly. He turned his head toward Samburu.

"Apologies, but I could not help but overhear your concerns of me being here."

Samburu looked at Bambara and frowned quizzically.

"Yes, why are you here?"

Bambara sighed and thought for a moment before responding. Images of the story he was about to share appeared in his mind with painful clarity. He prepared himself then began to tell the tale.

"I am here because the Ibos tribe in the north, allies to your friends the Spanish, attacked our caravan while we were on a pilgrimage to the sacred mountain, Kilimanjaro."

Vivid recollections streamed through Bambara's mind. He saw himself walking in front of a camel he pulled by the reins. He remembered the purple, full-length kente cloth tunic with matching pants he wore that day. His mother, Amhara, rode on the back of the camel he led wearing the same attire as he.

Behind them was a long line of Mandinka women. Most of them carrying large earthen jars on their heads, smiling and talking with one another, wearing beautiful kente cloth dresses. Mandinka children walked hand in hand, singing happily. They too were dressed correspondingly with bright green kente cloth tunics and pants.

An elderly couple smiled at one another as the Mandinka man pointed to Kilimanjaro in the distance with its snowcapped peak. Other elderly Mandinkas followed behind them. The men wore the same red kente cloth hats, shirts, and pants and the women wore corresponding red kente cloth dresses.

There were ten Mandinka warriors guarding the caravan, staggered on both sides of the narrow rocky road, as it snaked its way up towards the mountain. Each of them carried a spear and kept a watchful eye on the jungle to both sides of the road.

An Ibos warrior watched the caravan from a tree as it slowly moved by. His head was bald and painted with a white circle on top. The warrior concentrated on the caravan for a moment, then turned and looked down at the 50 Ibos warriors on the ground. He raised his hands swiftly and they all started to move through the jungle next to the caravan silently.

Amhara rode atop the camel and took in all of the natural beauty around her. She and Bambara smiled pleasantly as they talked to each other while making their way up the thin, red clay road carved through the jungle. Bambara pointed ahead at Kilimanjaro excitedly as it jutted up from the bottomland, still many miles away from where they were. Bambara remembered how he looked at the sacred mountain in awe and wonder.

Amhara placed her hand on her belly and smiled widely. She looked down at Bambara and pointed to her belly, ecstatically telling him that his brother had just kicked inside her.

Bambara stopped the camel immediately and turned towards his mother quickly. He reached up and placed his hand onto Amhara's belly gently. When he felt the strong kick of his baby brother he pulled his hand away, startled. They both looked at one another and burst into uncontrollable laughter.

Suddenly, Ibos warriors ran out from their hiding places in the jungle from both sides and attacked the caravan with devastating precision.

Bambara saw the Ibos attacking and pulled the dagger from its sheath on his right hip. He turned and faced the Ibos warrior barreling towards him and his mother. The Ibos swung his war club at Bambara's head. Bambara ducked his head low and skillfully dodged the club. He turned quickly and grabbed the Ibos warrior by the top of his head and with one swift move slit his throat from ear to ear. The warrior fell to the ground grabbing his throat as blood gurgled from the gash.

Blood sprayed onto Amhara's face. She closed her eyes, afraid. When she opened them again an Ibos warrior had a spear poised at her stomach. He turned his head sharply towards Bambara.

Bambara turned aggressively to continue to fight but saw his mother at the mercy of the Ibos warrior and reluctantly dropped his dagger to the ground. Bambara watched helplessly as his caravan was pillaged before his eyes.

Ten fearsome Ibos warriors clubbed the elderly Mandinkas. Each time they brought their war clubs down blood splattered into the air. The elderly Mandinka couple, who only moments before had been so excited about their pilgrimage, lay bludgeoned to death in a pool of their own blood, eyes open, looking at each other and still holding hands.

Ibos warriors tied the terrified, crying Mandinka children with rope around their hands and necks.

A Mandinka woman was dragged, kicking and screaming into the jungle by five Ibos warriors. She grabbed hold of a tree as they pulled her by it. Collectively, they tugged her by the legs and forced her to release the trunk of the tree. She reached out for help that would not come, as they carried her off and disappeared into the jungle. Bambara mentally returned to the present as he told his story.

"The caravan was mostly comprised of women, children and old ones. But that did not matter to them. They attacked us from all sides. It was a bloodbath. We did not have enough warriors to fight them off. The Ibos killed the old ones who would not be worth anything on the slave market..." he sighed then continued.

"The scum took the women and children, including mother and myself. My mother was worth more to them because she was with child and a royal. She made me swear not to reveal my true identity, so that they would not separate us."

Bambara hung his head and fought back tears. "So I did what she asked."

Fulani hung on every word of Bambara's tale with tears in her eyes.

Chief Yoruba listened intently, enthralled with the story as he took another gulp from his goblet.

Samburu removed a jug from the table and filled his goblet, then placed it back onto the table.

Bambara struggled to keep his emotions in check. He paused, took a deep breath and continued his tale of woe, as he relived it in his head.

"We were taken to the Portuguese Fort, *Sao Jorge Da Mina*." The bald Ibos warrior led the camel to the coastal fort with Amhara riding on back of it sobbing.

"The fort was bustling with human activity. Hundreds of captured Africans were being led into the fort, tied together by thick ropes around their necks and hands behind their backs. A Portuguese guard whipped an African man tied to a post just below the front gate of the fort.

"I lifted my head and witnessed Portuguese sentries on the wall grab their crotches and blow kisses disrespectfully at my mother. My neck and hands were tied to a string of young Mandinka warriors. I was defenseless."

"Amhara looked back at me, sobbing helplessly. I hid my identity from them and the Ibos sold us together to the Portuguese for metal pots, muskets and strong drink. They chained my mother and I together. Under the circumstances we both saw that as a small blessing until later that night. My mother was raped while I was chained right next to her."

Bambara broke down and covered his face with his hands. After a brief pause, he lowered his hands, cleared his throat and gathered himself.

Chief Yoruba waved for the servant girl to pour Bambara some wine. She quickly walked over to where Bambara was sitting and poured a healthy portion of wine into his cup, then walked back to her position.

Bambara lifted the cup to his lips and gulped down all of the contents. He nodded to the chief in appreciation.

"Thank you."

Bambara's thoughts returned to the painful details of the night his mother was violated beside him. He found himself lost in memories:

Outside, a lightning storm raged and the wind

howled. Inside, a damp and filthy dungeon floor cradled Bambara and Amhara, chained by the hands and neck beside one another. Amhara stared at the dungeon ceiling horrified, as she clutched her stomach.

Two Portuguese guards from the wall over the main gate entered the dungeon with torches to light their way. They stepped over many of the other slaves chained to the floor until they arrived to where Amhara was lying. The short and portly guard bent over Bambara's mother and quickly placed his hand over her mouth, as the tall stocky guard began to nervously unbutton his pants.

Amhara looked on in terror as she attempted to kick her feet at the stocky guard. She tried to scream, but it was muffled by the guard's hand. The tall guard pulled his pants to his ankles then pried Amhara's legs apart before thrusting his penis inside her. The portly guard kept his hand tightly over her mouth as his partner rammed her. He bent over and licked her face repeatedly.

Moments later, Bambara was awakened by the commotion next to him. Groggy, he turned his head in the direction of his mother and saw *her being raped. Horrified and disgusted, he attempted in vain to kick at the men, but to no avail.*

The tall guard thrust once more into Amhara and ejaculated, letting out a loud grunt as he did so, before jumping to his feet and pulling his pants up. The tall guard looked over at Bambara, who was kicking and spitting at him, trying to make as much noise as he could to alert someone. The tall guard stepped over Amhara and stomped Bambara's face with the heel of his boot and knocked him unconscious. He turned back to Amhara and placed his hand over her mouth, as the portly guard pulled his pants down.

Amhara kicked at the portly guard as he positioned himself to violate her. She successfully struck him in the groin with her right foot, sending him to the ground in pain.

The tall guard holding her mouth pointed and laughed at the portly guard. The guard she kicked in the groin looked down at Amhara furiously. He stood up, pulled his right leg back and kicked her in the stomach, over, and over, and over again, until Amhara coughed up blood and writhed in pain.

The two guards knew they would be in trouble for damaging precious cargo, so they quickly left the dungeon and closed the door behind them.

Bambara shook himself from his thoughts and continued with his story.

"I awoke and realized what was happening too late. I tried to kick at them. One of the guards stomped me unconscious. I wanted them to kill me, so I would not have to live with the shame of not being able to kill all the men who dishonored my mother. When I came to, I was aboard the Spanish slave ship, the *Matador*. My mother, chained next to me, was dead. I stared at her dead body for what had to be four days. I was able to escape only through the grace of Nyame, the all-seeing and all-knowing!" he said with great sorrow, as he returned mentally back to the present, unaware of the thick streams of tears running down his face.

Somewhat embarrassed at his emotional display, he abruptly stood and turned toward Chief Yoruba.

"Forgive me, my chief. But, my appetite seems to have left me. I must respectfully retire for the evening."

Bambara bowed his head to the chief and then left the hut without acknowledging anyone else in the hut.

Fulani wiped the tears from her face and thought for a moment before standing and quickly leaving the hut as well.

Samburu lifted his goblet to his mouth and took a sip from it. After placing it back on the table in front of him, he looked over at his father. "Well, that was a good story," he snickered sarcastically.

Chief Yoruba immediately shot a disapproving look at him, got up from the table and abruptly walked out.

CHAPTER 7

FUTURE KINGS
SHOULD NOT BE ON THEIR KNEES

Bambara stood silent by the river's edge. The moon eerily illuminated the jungle. He lifted his head to the sky and stared into the enormous full moon with tears rolling down his face. Slowly, he raised his hands to the moon as he fell reverently to his knees to pray.

"Nyame! Supreme God of the heavens! Creator of the three realms-- sky, earth, and underworld! I implore you, hear me now! It is I, your humble servant, Bambara of the Mandinka tribe. I pledge the ultimate sacrifice to you-- my own life-- if you grant me the gift of sight, so that I know what I must do is within your plan for me!" He shut his eyes tightly and dropped his head slowly.

Fulani appeared suddenly, walking slowly and seductively toward Bambara by the river.

"Future kings should not be on their knees!"

she yelled as she walked towards him, seductively disrobing while crossing the damp sand of the training circle.

Startled, Bambara turned his head and body around swiftly. He could not believe what he was witnessing, as he watched the princess removing articles of her clothing. Slowly, he stood, not taking his eyes off of Fulani for a second.

"Fulani, it is late! What are you doing here? Is your father upset with me because I left so abruptly?" He shouted nervously.

"I will apologize to him in the morning!"

The light of the moon hit Fulani's perfectly fit body. She stopped in the light intentionally to give Bambara the total view of her curvaceous physique, which was revealed through the sheer fabric of her remaining garment.

Bambara wantonly studied her every curve.

Fulani again moved toward Bambara, removing the final sheer garment from her shoulders and delicately dropped it to the ground, becoming completely naked as she came face-to-face with Bambara.

He peered deeply into her eyes bursting with

passion for her.

The princess gazed deeply into the eyes of Bambara, as she began to tug on and unwrap his loincloth. After a few quick tugs, she allowed the loincloth to fall to the ground, revealing his chiseled buttocks. Fulani began to gently stroke his throbbing manhood with her right hand, while she continued to stare into his eyes.

Unable to stand it for another moment, Bambara took Fulani's face into his hands and gently pulled her to him. He kissed her lips passionately as if it was the last time he would be able to have her.

Fulani pulled her face away from Bambara's, but continued to look into his eyes seductively. "You are my king... so I fall to my knees, for you, and only for you."

Fulani dropped slowly to her knees, softly kissing Bambara's chest as she descended.

Bambara closed his eyes and leaned his head back in ecstasy, as the feel of her soft, gentle mouth stirred his loins into a frenzy. He had never known such pleasure until that very moment.

As the sun rose the next morning, Bambara

and Fulani lay naked in the grass by the river in each other's embrace. Bambara opened his eyes and smiled when he saw Fulani lying next to him. He reached behind himself and plucked a long blade of grass from the ground. He took it and gently ran it across Fulani's face playfully. Fulani crinkled her face, but did not awaken. He ran the blade of grass over her face once more.

She swatted at the blade of grass with her left hand and opened her eyes. Fulani saw the blade of grass in Bambara's hand and smiled widely before kissing him.

"I thought last night was a dream. I find myself very relieved, that it was not," Bambara confessed.

"No. It was no dream, Mandinka. Your story, the story about your mother... you did something to me that no other man has been able to do."

Bambara's curiosity peaked, as he looked at Fulani intrigued.

"What was that, Princess?"

Fulani took a deep breath of moist, crisp morning air, then turned away from Bambara, thinking of his heartwrenching story from the night before.

"You moved me, Bambara of the Mandinka. You moved me," she answered in her most sincere of voices. Fulani rolled closer to Bambara and kissed him on the forehead before she jumped to her feet and scrambled around picking her garments off the ground.

Bambara reveled in the taste of her soft lips for a moment before he rolled onto his belly smiling as he watched Fulani scramble naked from place to place, retrieving her garments. Fulani giggled happily as she quickly reclaimed her clothing from the ground.

"I must return to my father's house before I am missed. It would not be good for you, or I, if they discovered I've lain with a lowly Mandinkan Prince! That simply would not do!" she giggled.

"I will see you at training later!" Fulani struggled to put her clothing on quickly.

"I must hurry!"

Bambara stood then walked over to where Fulani was getting dressed. He took her by the hands and raised them softly to his mouth and kissed them gently before bringing them down to his chest. He looked deeply into Fulani's eyes.

Fulani looked back at Bambara strangely, before she broke into a wide smile. She placed her right hand onto her stomach and reminisced about the evening she had with him.

"My stomach feels like there have been a thousand butterflies released into it. It feels funny," she said just before she turned and ran across the training circle smiling from ear to ear.

"I'll see you later, Bambara!"

Bambara watched Fulani run across the training circle. He watched until she disappeared over the hill. Bambara lifted his head to the sky, closed his eyes and raised both his arms humbly. "I thank you, Nyame, the All Powerful, for answering my prayer! I know now that my mission has your blessing, oh Mighty One!"

He lowered his head and walked back to his hut.

CHAPTER 8

TRAINING DAY

Bambara looked on as the members of the Mortisi trained at the various apparatuses in the training circle. The sun's rays heated the sand of the circle up to nearly 100 degrees.

Two Mortisi warriors wrestled in the one-on-one combat ring in the center of the training circle. One warrior skillfully hip threw another to the ground. The Mortisi warrior, who was thrown to the ground, swiftly wrapped his legs around the leg of the warrior who had hip thrown him and brought him to the ground using a leg hold.

Adangbe knelt next to the wooden wall in another area of the circle. He cupped his hands and intertwined his fingers.

Ten Mortisi warriors stood in a single file line hanging on Adangbe's every word. Adangbe motioned with his hands, signaling the first warrior to run toward him. The first warrior ran as fast as he could toward Adangbe and placed his right foot into Adangbe's awaiting hands. He stood and lifted the warrior to the top of the wall. The warrior scaled the rest of the wall with ease and dropped to the other side. The next Mortisi warrior in line did the exact same thing as the first.

Bambara turned his head in the direction of Fulani. She stood at arm's-length from a tree stump that had been debarked. Her arms had been fashioned onto the sides of the apparatus. Wearing her Tutsi sickle knives on her back, she moved around the apparatus slowly, as she concentrated.

Suddenly, with cat-like reflexes, she pulled her weapons from behind her head and struck the apparatus with her sickle knives in both hands. She struck so swiftly, that her weapons were barely visible to the naked eye as she struck again and again. She twirled her weapons in each hand then struck. She spun her body around and struck again. Fulani moved around the entire apparatus and struck it in the front, the back, and both sides, before backflipping away from it, landing in a full split and returning her sickle knives into their harness behind her head in seemingly one motion.

Fulani was breathing heavily, so she closed her eyes and focused on slowing it down by breathing smoothly through her nose and exhaling from her mouth.

Bambara smiled as he scanned his warriors around the circle.

"Very good, my Mortisi!" he shouted proudly. Bambara motioned for everyone to come to him with his hands.

Adangbe, Fulani, and the other Mortisi warriors ran to where Bambara was standing. They formed a square formation in front of Bambara, four warriors across and five lines deep.

"We have to be the most fit, most skilled and most determined warriors in this land. We took a huge leap into that direction today. I will see you all tomorrow to continue!"

Suddenly, Samburu interrupted with a contingent of his bodyguards behind him. "Bambara! May I have a word?"

Bambara and Fulani looked at one another suspiciously. Bambara turned into Samburu's direction and slowly walked toward him.

Adangbe attempted to go with Bambara, but Bambara turned his head slightly to him.

"Adangbe, it will be all right. I will go alone my brother."

Adangbe stood down as he was ordered and returned to the ranks of the Mortisi.

Samburu walked nonchalantly down the hill toward Bambara until they met on the side of the hill. Samburu looked at the Mortisi standing stoically in formation.

"Your warriors look eager to fight for you, Mandinka," he said sarcastically.

"Is that not a warrior's job, my Prince?" replied Bambara, equally as sarcastic.

Samburu smiled.

"Bambara, I have come here to apologize for my childish behavior. After you told us your incredible story, I felt ashamed of my attitude towards you. Could you find it in your heart to forgive me for being a pompous ass?"

Bambara was totally taken aback. He looked at Samburu surprised. He thought for a moment then reached out his hand and they shook each other's forearms for the first time.

"I must apologize as well, for being so reactionary, Prince Samburu."

Fulani glanced up at the two of them making peace with one another. She smiled uncontrollably as she watched Bambara and her brother shake.

"That was nothing. Let us put all of that foolishness behind us. I have another gift for you besides my friendship," Samburu added.

"A gift? The prince is too kind," Bambara quipped suspiciously.

Samburu smiled slyly and held his right pointer finger into the air.

"Hold on. Before you accept this, know that you will be responsible for protecting me. You, and your Mortisi, that is if you think your men are up to the challenge?"

Excitedly Bambara replied, "Yes, my prince! It will be an honor for the Mortisi to protect you in any way!"

Samburu smirked and bowed his head half-heartedly. Then he turned and walked back up the hill towards his bodyguards. Once at the top, he turned his head slightly and yelled down to Bambara.

"I will be expecting you and your men in the morning ready to escort me to the coast!"

Bambara looked down at his hands and slowly balled them into fists. He turned and faced Fulani, Adangbe, and the rest of his warriors and shouted, "The Mortisi has received its first mission! We will have the honor of being the sole protection for the prince of the mighty Ashanti!"

The Mortisi warriors let out a collective yell in celebration of the news.

Fulani watched Bambara celebrating on the hill and smiled widely, as she too joined in the merriment and began to dance joyously.

With a concerned scowl upon his face, Adangbe looked around at the celebrating members of the Mortisi. He raised his head up to where Bambara was dancing and started walking towards him. Once he was a few feet away from Bambara, Adangbe shouted to him in a serious tone.

"What is this mission for the Mortisi, my Commander?"

Caught up in his own amusement, Bambara continued to dance until he looked up and saw the expression on Adangbe's face. He stopped dancing and approached his captain.

"Our mission is to escort Prince Samburu to the coast, where he has business, I assume!"

Adangbe thought for a moment, as Bambara returned to his celebratory dance. Adangbe stopped thinking and asked another question.

"The coast? Why are we going to the coast? For what purpose?"

Bambara snapped his head around in anger. "For what? This is none of your concern! It is for the Mortisi to follow without question! I thought you, of all my warriors who gave their oaths, understood that!"

Fulani and the other warriors stopped celebrating when they heard Bambara's outburst and turned their heads towards him and Adangbe on the hill. Adangbe fell to his knees and lowered his head apologetically.

"Forgive me, my prince. My only motive for questioning the mission is to protect you from you enemies," he looked up at him in earnest humbleness, "Foreign and domestic, Commander!"

Bambara slowly broke into a smile as he

looked down on Adangbe. He stepped over to him and grabbed him by the shoulders, then lifted him to his feet.

"I know what your motives are, my friend. With you watching my back, I fear nothing. Apologies, my friend for being so overbearing. I am just relishing this opportunity to prove what we can do in battle!"

Adangbe and Bambara both smile and nod to one another. Both men turned simultaneously and began walking down the hill towards the others.

As he approached Fulani, Bambara smiled at her lovingly. She smiled back in the same manner then became serious.

"So, you and my brother have become friends?" she asked concerned.

"It would appear so."

Bambara grabbed Fulani by the hands and peered into her eyes and spoke low so none of the others would hear.

"When can I be with you again?"

Fulani blushed. "I'm not sure, but we have to be very, very careful." she whispered then kissed him on the cheek before sprinting toward the kraal! Bambara watched her as she disappeared over the hill.

Near the center of the kraal, Samburu strolled confidently ahead of his bodyguards. Fulani ran until she caught up to them and stopped right in front of her brother. He stopped and smiled slyly at her.

"Sister! How are you?

"I am fine, brother. This mission we are to go on tomorrow, is it real?" she prodded with desperate concern.

Samburu laughed and stepped toward Fulani, placing his arm around her as he whispered in her ear.

"Careful, little sister. One might get the wrong impression about you and the Mandinka's relationship."

Fulani pulled away from Samburu and gave him an appalled look. Disgusted, she rebutted.

"What are you trying to imply, brother?"

Samburu grabbed his belly as he laughed hardily once more.

"I'm implying nothing. Just that I've never seen you react this way to someone, I mean in the way you do with this man, that's all. I'm sorry if I have made you cross with me. I only want you to remember who you are, sister! That's all I am really saying... remember... who... you... are!"

Fulani calmed herself and forced a fake smile.

"So what time are we to leave?"

Samburu looked at Fulani surprised.

"We? Do you mean *you*? Oh no sister, you cannot come with us. It will be too dangerous. Besides, father would never allow it!"

Fulani grew angry instantly.

"Huh! We'll see about that! I am not a child anymore! I am Mortisi, just like the rest of them! I took an oath and will break it for no one! Not even you, beloved brother!"

Then she turned and walked away from Samburu and his men stoically.

Samburu turned to the head of his bodyguards and looked at him suspiciously. He turned back quickly into the direction Fulani walked and shouted to her.

"Fulani, wait!"

Hearing her brother's call, she stopped and turned. Samburu trotted up to her.

"Don't be angry with me, sister. I could not

bare that. I'm only trying to protect you."

"Protect me? Protect me from what, brother? You've been away for a long time. If you saw my skill on the battlefield, you would know that I need no protection. My enemies need protection from me!"

Samburu thought to himself for a moment, then lifted his head and raised his arms simultaneously in concession.

"All right! You win! You can go. But I'm not going to be the one to tell father. That job will fall on your pretty little head."

Fulani could hardly contain her emotions. She felt as if she were about to burst with joy. She jumped up and down like a child, then grabbed Samburu and hugged him as tight as she could.

"Thank you! Oh, thank you, brother! You will not regret this, I swear! Thank you!"

Fulani finally released her brother and ran as fast as she could toward Chief Yoruba's hut. Samburu and his bodyguards began to walk again. He heard Fulani's voice fade away as she entered the chief's hut.

"Father! Father! Where are you, father?"

Inside his dwelling Chief Yoruba sat at his

table eating from a plate of fruit. Fulani ran over to him at the table beside herself with excitement.

"Father, I have the greatest news!"

The chief wiped his mouth with a piece of cloth and looked up a Fulani confused.

"What is this news, Fulani? Are you getting married by any chance?" he quipped sarcastically before smiling playfully at her.

Fulani twisted her lips up and rolled her eyes playfully at her father, then moved closer to him and jumped into his lap. She twirled his beard under his chin with her right pointer finger as she shared her news.

"No, I am not getting married! I and the other Mortisi are going on our first official mission in the morning!"

Chief Yoruba's demeanor changed from jovial to serious in an instant.

"A mission? What kind of mission, and under whose authority?"

Fulani stood and looked at her father concerned by his attitude.

"Our mission is to escort Samburu to the coast. He has some type of business to take care of there."

Chief Yoruba stood and thought hard, wearing a scowl.

"It is strange that your brother did not mention any such mission to me. Well, then again, he might have mentioned it while I had been drinking!" He laughed, then turned and hugged Fulani and looked into her eyes.

"Being as though you are a far superior warrior than your brother, be sure that he returns home safely."

The chief kissed Fulani on the forehead lovingly and smiled proudly at her.

"On my life, I promise I will bring Samburu home, father."

Chief Yoruba walked back over to his chair and sat back down. He looked up at Fulani with tears in his eyes.

"Your mother would have been so proud of you, little one."

Before his daughter could see him cry, he quickly lowered his head and began to eat once more. Fulani thought on her father's words then left his hut.

CHAPTER 9

FIRST MISSION

Samburu and Bambara walked side by side down the main road from the kraal. The kraal was miles away from where they had traveled to, but could still be seen in the distance behind them. Both of them walked at the head of twenty Mortisi warriors all garbed in thin black leather loincloths. Each man carried spears in their right hands and black bows across their backs, with arrows in pouches under their left arms.

Fulani, the only woman, marched proudly in the ranks of the Mortisi. She was wearing the same black leather loincloth as the men, but also had her breasts covered with a matching black leather top. The handles of her Tutsi sickle knives stuck out on both sides of her head, but she carried a Mortisi spear as well.

Bambara turned and snuck a quick peek at Fulani.

Fulani noticed him looking and motioned

with her head for him to turn around.

Samburu glanced over at Bambara and sees him staring at his sister, but ignores it.

"We should be at the coast by nightfall at this pace. What do you think, Bambara?"

Bambara snapped his head back around. "I think my prince is correct. If my prince would rather we get there faster, my Mortisi shall go at any pace you command, faster, if you so wish it."

Samburu chuckled.

"No, that won't be necessary, Bambara... this pace will do."

Bambara bowed his head toward Samburu and continued at the same pace.

By nightfall, their party had reached the coast. In the harbor were anchored two large sailing ships. Samburu, Bambara, Fulani, and the Mortisi marched over the last sand dune before the whole of the pristine harbor came into their view. They discovered multiple fire sites dotting the darkening beach in front of them, with many sailors congregated and warming themselves by the firesides.

Bambara waved his left hand forward and

signaled for Adangbe.

Adangbe quickly ran to where Bambara stood at the head of their formation.

"Be sure everyone is alert," Bambara ordered in an intense tone.

Adangbe nodded, then returned to his place in the ranks.

Samburu smirked slyly as he made his way down the dune. He stopped suddenly and turned to Bambara.

"Neither you nor your men are to say a word. I will handle all negotiations, is that clear?"

Bambara hesitated, then, answered.

"Yes, my prince."

Samburu smiled sinisterly. "Excellent!"

He turned once more and continued to trudge down the sand dune toward the vessels' encampment on the beach.

Samburu, Bambara, and Fulani, followed by the rest of the Mortisi, marched apprehensively into the center of the seamens' camp.

Bambara craned his head from side to side as he kept a watchful eye on the crewmen to both sides of them warming themselves by the campfires.

Adangbe walked cautiously through the camp gripping his spear tightly in both hands.

The crewmen stared with disdain at Bambara and the Mortisi. Some spit in their direction as a sign of disrespect.

Fulani looked over at four sailors sitting by one of the campfires. One of the men sitting closest to the area in which she was walking exposed his tongue at her in a vulgar manner. She quickly snapped her head back into the direction she and the others were walking.

The vulgar crewman slapped his friend on the shoulder and they all laughed about his gesture.

Soon they came upon a tall Caucasian man in his forties who was warming his hands in a campfire at the very center of the encampment. He wore a large black three-point hat. His hair was long, sun bleached and wild. The man was also handsome with about three days of stubble on his face. He raised his head and saw Samburu making his way towards him. The man smiled widely. He stood then walked around to the other side of the fire to meet Samburu. Then, in a thick Southern drawl he addressed Samburu, "Welcome, Prince Samburu! Welcome!"

Samburu walked up to Captain Bishop and smiled as he extended his hand to him. The two men shook hands. Samburu peeked over the right shoulder of the captain. Speaking English with a thick African accent, Samburu queried. "Where is Captain Fletcher? It was my understanding that he would be a part of our business transaction?"

Captain Bishop hesitated for a moment before answering.

"Uh... Captain Fletcher was not feeling up to coming ashore. He has been a bit under the weather, Your Highness! But he has instructed me to assure you that this will not deter our business today. The captain awaits us aboard the *Carolina Gold*! He's not one for spending too much time on land anyway," he answered in a shady manner.

Captain Bishop turned and clapped his hands twice. Immediately, two husky African slaves carried a large crate from the beach and sat it next to the campfire where they all were standing.

Captain Bishop turned his head and grinned at Samburu. He pointed at the crate.

"The captain did instruct me to bring this crate of brand new muskets, for your inspection, of course!"

Bambara and Adangbe glanced at one another suspiciously then turned back towards Samburu and Captain Bishop.

Fulani scanned around the camp nervously.

Samburu flipped the lid of the crate open, like a kid at Christmas. He bent down and picked one of the muskets out of the crate. He lowered his face to it and inhaled deeply smelling the oil inside the breech, as if smelling a flower. He turned toward Bambara and smiled as he placed the musket back into the crate. Samburu reached down and grabbed a fistful of sand then rubbed his hands together to rid them of the residue from the oil.

"Your Captain Fletcher seems to be a man who can be trusted," Samburu told Captain Bishop, pleased.

Captain Bishop nodded to one of the husky slaves.

The slave turned and lifted a small wooden box off the ground behind him. He walked to where Samburu and Captain Bishop were standing and extended the box toward Samburu.

Samburu looked at the captain pleasantly surprised.

Captain Bishop smiled widely as he opened the box and revealed a large solid gold clock inside.

"This is just a small sample of what we have for you, my prince. My country and I have longed to find a strong and reliable ally here in West Africa!"

Samburu marveled at the gold clock, as he gently ran his fingers over it.

Fulani, Bambara, and Adangbe stood with mouths agape as they stared in wonder at the marvelously crafted, sparkling timepiece.

"What is this beautiful trinket?"

Samburu asked, as he studied his gift further.

"It is called a clock, your majesty. It is used to tell the time of day," said Captain Bishop.

Fulani walked over to Samburu and marveled at the solid gold clock. She touched it delicately, as if it would shatter if she did not take care.

Captain Bishop studied Fulani as she played with the clock. He studied every inch of her, from the bulging muscles in her arms, to her chiseled legs and ripped abdomen.

"There is more treasure where that came from on my ship, Your Highness. This is but one of the many gifts that my associates and I will present you with on this night," continued the captain.

Samburu, irritated, scowled displeased with Captain Bishop. "The gold was supposed to be on the beach when I arrived, Captain! That was the arrangement!"

The crewmen within an earshot of where the negotiation was happening started to murmur about Samburu's tone and some stood aggressively.

Bambara saw some of the crewmen stand and immediately ordered the Mortisi in military fashion.

"Protect!"

He and the Mortisi formed a half circle around Samburu, then turned and faced the threatening crewman and poised their spears towards them simultaneously.

Fulani snatched her Tutsi Sickle knives from behind her head with both hands blindingly fast and stood poised beside her Mortisi brothers at the ready.

Samburu smiled at the captain smugly.

"As you see, my Mortisi will protect me to the last. Are you able to make the same claim for all of your men here, Captain?"

Captain Bishop, concerned, raised his hands in the air to calm his men down.

"Hey now! Everyone calm down. Boys, everything is all right! Let's everybody just calm the hell down! This night is about making new friends, not enemies!"

He chuckled.

The crewmen mumbled amongst one another, then began to sit around their fires again.

Samburu looked toward Bambara and calmly ordered him in African. "Stand down."

Bambara repeated the order to the Mortisi. "Stand down." The Mortisi in perfect unison brought their spears to rest at their sides.

Captain Bishop watched Fulani specifically as she returned her sickle knives to their holders on her back. Lustfully, he said one word under his breath in reaction to Fulani.

"Magnificent!"

Samburu turned to Captain Bishop confused.

"What was that?"

Captain Bishop intentionally evaded Samburu's question.

"I would've had my men bring the rest of the gold to shore but, then you would have to worry about all of the other savages... excuse me, Your Highness, what I meant to say was, the other tribes in the area sniffing around. Besides, all that gold is heavy, you understand? So, what we should do is hop into the longboats and make our way to the ship. I'm sure Captain Fletcher is wondering by now what's keeping us."

Samburu grinned, then followed Captain Bishop towards the longboats on the beach, which were manned by four crewmen with oars in each of them.

Bambara walked quickly up to Samburu and grabbed him by the arm concerned. "Prince Samburu, I hope you are not planning to go aboard this barbarian's ship?"

Samburu snatched his arm away from him. "Yes, I do plan to go on that ship! The rest of what I came here for is on it! Oh, is the mighty Mandinka afraid of the white man's ship?" he asked condescendingly.

Bambara answered in the most sincere way he could.

"Yes, with everything in me. I do not trust these men, my prince!"

Captain Bishop turned and saw Samburu and Bambara conversing.

"Is there a problem, your majesty?"

Samburu turned and forced a smile. "No captain! There is no problem. Shall we... how do you say, shove off?"

He snapped his head back around and stared into the face of Bambara.

"You and your men will do what I say, is this or is this not what you swore your oath upon?"

Bambara sighed in disappointment.

"Yes, my prince."

"So, do as I command!"

Samburu turned and moved toward the longboats again.

Bambara was troubled with concern, as he watched Samburu climb into one of the boats on shore. Hearing Samburu's words echo in his head about the oaths that he and his men had sworn, he reluctantly raised his right hand and signaled for the Mortisi to head toward the longboats as well. Before climbing into one of the small crafts, he turned and grabbed Fulani by the arm and whispered into her ear.

"Stay close to me when we go to the ship, and please keep your eyes open."

Fulani nodded with an intense look, then continued toward to the boat.

Captain Bishop stared at Fulani as she walked to the same boat that he was in. He extended his right hand to help her into it. She ignored his hand and took a seat beside her brother.

Once all of the Mortisi were in the boats, the crewmen on the boats shoved off and began to row toward the ships in the harbor.

CHAPTER 10

THE CAROLINA GOLD

Once the longboats grew close to the ship, Bambara, Fulani, and the others heard sounds of an unfamiliar instrument vigorously being played on deck. They also heard multiple hands clapping joyously in rhythm to the music.

Captain Bishop was the first to climb the thick rope ladder up the side of the ship. Once at the top of the ladder, he jumped down to the deck with a huge smile on his face before he turned and looked down at Samburu and his men.

Bambara and Adangbe climbed up next. When they reached the top of the rope ladder, they jumped onto the deck and quickly surveyed the situation.

Both of them were not prepared for what they saw. Many scantily clad African women from different tribes and Caucasian women were dancing around a few white crewmen sitting on the deck of the ship. At the center of all the merriment was Captain Fletcher, an overweight, full-bearded man with a large black three-point hat on his head. He was unhealthy looking and drank from a metal cup, spilling half the contents down his beard and onto his shirt. Captain Fletcher wiped his beard with his left hand and continued to enjoy the view and music as he laughed hardily.

The musician, who supplied the music from the fiddle, was a dashingly handsome young white man around eighteen or nineteen years of age. He slid the bow over the strings of his fiddle skillfully as he walked around the audience on deck smiling and playing up to the crowd.

A few other crewmen sat close to one another accompanying the fiddler with a stand up bass, banjo, and guitar. They too were all smiling and enjoying playing together.

Samburu, Fulani, and the other Mortisi jumped onto the deck behind Bambara and Adangbe. They all marveled at the fiddler as he went from person to person playing in front of them.

Captain Fletcher bent forward in order to see

around the person who was seated next to him and saw the contingent. He smiled widely and took a long swig from the cup he had in his right hand. Again, he wiped his mouth with his left shirtsleeve and stood facing the direction of the contingent.

"Ahoy there!" he yelled jovially toward Samburu and his contingent then motioned for them to come closer. Captain Fletcher kicked the crewman next to him off the box he was sitting on and adjusted the custom shotgun pistols he was wearing on his waist before walking towards Samburu, Bambara and the others. Bambara stared at the custom pistols on Captain Fletcher's waist. Captain Bishop grinned as Captain Fletcher approached.

"Please allow me to welcome you all to the *Carolina Gold*!"

Captain Bishop shook Captain Fletcher's hand.

"Captain Fletcher, sir... please allow me the honor of introducing his Royal Highness, Prince Samburu of the Ashanti Empire."

Captain Fletcher wiped his right hand on his pant leg then reached out to shake Samburu's hand. Samburu nodded and smiled as he shook the captain's hand. Captain Fletcher looked over at the Mortisi.

"I see you've brought the whole village with you!" he laughed loudly.

Samburu remained stone faced as Captain Fletcher continued.

"Let us find you a comfortable place to sit, Your Highness. A place befitting your station, of course."

Captain Fletcher, Captain Bishop, Samburu, Bambara, and Fulani walked slowly to the area in which Captain Fletcher was seated earlier. A few moments later, two of the dancing girls sauntered over to Samburu, much to his surprise. The women took him by both arms and guided him away from the others, smiling.

The instruments that the colorless men played intrigued Mortisi. They cautiously walked over to the musicians and without warning grabbed the guitar and banjo from the crewmen's hands, stopping the accompaniment instantly. The crewmen, who lost their instruments to the Mortisi, backed away graciously as Adangbe and the others inspected their instruments thoroughly.

Bambara looked around the deck of the ship suspiciously. The young man playing the fiddle stopped playing and walked over to Bambara. He smiled as he extended his hand to him. Bambara glanced down at the fiddler's hand, unsure if he should take it.

The fiddler felt uncomfortable, so he lowered his hand a bit embarrassed. An uncomfortable silence of a few seconds followed before the fiddler pointed to himself.

"Hello... my name is Simon," he spoke slowly and deliberately, not knowing if Bambara could understand. Bambara continued to stare at Simon suspiciously.

"Si... mon, that is my name," he continued while pointing at himself again.

Samburu burst into hysterical laughter.

"I'm afraid my escorts do not speak the language of the Americas," Samburu announced smugly. Simon nodded to Bambara respectfully and walked away. Captain Bishop turned his head in the direction of Simon.

"Hey boy! Play another tune for our honored guests!"

Samburu turned to Captain Fletcher.

"Captain Fletcher, I was told that the rest of my cargo was here aboard your ship!"

The captain turned to Samburu.

"Actually, Your Highness, your cargo is on Captain Bishop's ship. But, we'll have plenty of time to deal with that. How about for now, you relax and enjoy yourself? Take time to get to know as many of the girls as you'd like, Prince Samburu."

Captain Fletcher lifted a brown jug off the deck and passed it to Captain Bishop. He drank from it and passed the jug to Samburu.

Samburu hesitantly took the jug from Captain Bishop. He sighed then drank from the jug. He gulped down the strong liquid as fast as he could, careful not to let on that he thought it tasted horrible, before passing the jug back to Captain Bishop.

Captain Fletcher pulled a skinny gold pipe from his coat. He looked up at one of the dancing girls. The girl didn't notice the captain's gaze at first, but when she saw him waiting, she quickly made her way over to him and lit his pipe with a match that she pulled from inside the top of her dress. Captain Fletcher reared back in his chair, lifted his head and blew out the rest of the smoke from his mouth. Smiling, he turned his head toward Captain Bishop before handing his pipe to him.

Captain Bishop took the pipe delicately with both hands and passed it to Samburu, who placed it into his mouth and took a long inhale. He lifted his head back and blew a large white smoke cloud from his mouth. His head began to feel a bit strange-- in an unusually good way. He smiled before turning his head toward a disapproving Bambara. Still smiling, Samburu signaled with his right hand for Bambara to come to him. Bambara and Adangbe looked on uncomfortably while Samburu's attention shifted towards the dancing girls.

Bambara slowly walked over to where Fulani was standing while simultaneously keeping an eye on everything that was going on.

"Stay sharp," he urged under his breath.

Fulani nodded to him.

Slowly, Bambara made his way over to where Samburu, Captain Fletcher and Captain Bishop were sitting. He stopped behind Samburu and bent at the waist, and whispered in his ear.

"Yes, my prince."

Samburu took the pipe from Captain Bishop and passed it to Bambara.

"You are too tense my friend, you must learn to relax! Can you not tell, we are amongst friends here?"

He held the pipe up to Bambara.

"Take this... and smoke it! That is an order, Mandinka," demanded Samburu.

Bambara glanced over at a concerned Fulani. Samburu noticed the glance and became angry.

"Why are you looking at my sister? You do realize that as long as I draw breath, I will never allow you to be with her? Now smoke!"

Bambara reluctantly took the pipe from Samburu's hands, placed it into his mouth and took a long toke. He closed his eyes before coughing puffs of white smoke from his mouth. He attempted to return the pipe to a much disoriented Samburu, who was at that point ranting incoherently.

"I want all of you to try this, uuuuh... this uuuuh... Haha, Captain Bishop?" he asked.

"What are we smoking? What is it called?"

Captain Bishop smiled at Samburu sinisterly. When answering Samburu's question, he spoke to him as if speaking to a small child.

"Opium, Your Highness. What you are smoking is called opium! From what I hear it is all the rage in England these days!"

Bambara turned slowly and started to walk toward Adangbe. Suddenly, his vision became very blurry and an involuntary euphoria came over him. Bambara stumbled to Adangbe and passed the pipe to him.

"See that all of the men try some of this. It is magical and quite stimulating," he said while wearing a silly grin on his face.

Captain Fletcher moved his head and signaled the most beautiful dancing girl on the deck of the ship to make a move on Bambara. Her beauty was only matched by her voluptuousness.

The beautiful dancing girl walked seductively towards Bambara. She danced in front of him as she unbuttoned the tight blouse she wore, freeing her ample breasts from restraint, exposing them. Bambara's eyes studied her body with lustful eyes.

Fulani looked on angrily, filled with

jealously. Frustrated, she stomped over to where Samburu had his head under one of the dancer's dresses, kissing her private area. She lifted the dancer's dress and pulled her brother's head from between the dancer's legs. Samburu looked up at Fulani delirious from the drug.

"What do you think you are doing, sister? Why are you not enjoying yourself?"

He turned his head and looked over at Bambara who was sucking on the ample breasts of the beautiful black dancer. He turned back to Fulani and burst into mocking laughter.

"Oh... I guess not!"

Fulani, determined to get all of her people off of the ship before further incident, tried to refocus her brother on the task at hand.

"Let us get what we have come for and leave this place, brother!"

Irritated, Samburu rebutted.

"All right, all right, sister! You sound like mother used to when we were in trouble, but you're right. Let us get to the task at hand. I am truly sorry, captains, but my sister is not enjoying herself, so I must insist that we conclude our affairs!"

Adangbe stealthily backed himself up to the rail of the ship. He scanned the deck keeping a watchful eye on the activities taking place. He rested his back on the rail and took a deep breath trying to clear his head. Suddenly, a rope was thrown around his neck from below the rail he was leaning against; it tightened as he was pulled backwards over the side of the ship.

Captain Bishop stood and addressed Samburu.

"Perhaps your sister would like to partake in some of the dragon's tail as well?"

Fulani scowled and rolled her eyes at Captain Bishop. She turned and stared at Samburu. Samburu stood, but was so disoriented that he almost fell back to the deck. He regained his balance and turned to the captains.

"Captain Bishop, if you would be so kind as to escort us to your ship, so that I can claim the rest of my cargo? That sir, would be greatly appreciated."

Captain Bishop stood and tipped his three-pointed hat politely to Fulani and smiled.

"It would be my pleasure, Your Highness. Come with me and I will square you away. Hey,

I have an outstanding idea. Why don't you bring your sister along? I'm sure I have a beautiful dress or two I am most positive she would love."

Samburu smiled and drank the remainder of the liquor in his cup.

"That is very kind of you, Captain."

Captain Bishop continued to stare at Fulani lustfully.

"Oh, it is no problem, Prince Samburu, I assure you. No problem at all."

Samburu stood and grinned at Fulani.

"You will come with me, sister! I need your protection while we go to retrieve my cargo."

Fulani searched around the deck for Bambara. When she finally located him, her heart fell as if it would burst inside of her chest. Bambara had the beautiful dancer bent over holding onto the bottom of the main mast to steady herself as he violently pounded her from behind. With each thrust from him the dancer moaned loudly for all to hear.

The rest of the Mortisi were in similar states of debauchery. After smoking from the opium pipe, not one of them was coherent enough to pay attention to what was going on. Each one was distracted by one of the women provided by the captains.

Fulani took one more look at Bambara and the dancer having violent intercourse. She tried as hard as she could to conceal her heartache but was unable to control her emotions. Her eyes swelled and tears began to stream down her face. She quickly wiped them and tried her best to recompose herself.

Samburu and Captain Bishop began to walk towards the side of the ship where the rope ladder was located. Captain Bishop descended the ladder first, followed by Samburu, then Fulani, who paused at the top of the rope ladder to take one more look at Bambara.

Bambara climaxed hard and violently into the dancer, who cried out in complete and utter ecstasy. Out of breath, he turned his head to the right and saw Fulani staring at him from over the rail of the ship. He shook his head, attempting to clear it. In a brief moment of clarity he could see Fulani heartbroken with her eyes full of tears. Bambara, realizing what he had done, lowered his head in shame. Fulani took a deep breath and descended the rope ladder quickly.

Seeing the look on Fulani's face sobered Bambara immediately. He looked around the deck and saw his Mortisi being plied with drink. Some were smoking from the opium pipe and others were having sex openly on the deck with the dancers. His vision blurry, Bambara squinted and saw Captain Fletcher walking to the bridge of the ship. Bambara searched the deck for Adangbe but could not locate him.

He turned his attention back to Captain Fletcher who stopped and stood behind the large steering wheel of the ship. He struggled to focus as the beautiful dancer placed her arms around him once more and kissed him passionately. Unable to fight the effects of the drugs, he kissed her back passionately and they both dropped slowly to the deck once more.

While Bambara and the rest of the Mortisi were being distracted, four crewmen from the ship arose from their seats on deck and quietly made their way to the cathead located at the bow of the ship. Once there, each of them took hold of one of the wooden arms protruding from the cathead and began to push the arms counterclockwise circularly. As they did so, the thick chain connected to the anchor began to ascend from the water.

Captain Fletcher sharply spun the ship's wheel to the left as soon as the anchor had become visible from beneath the murky water. The huge vessel creaked and swayed as it lumbered out to the open ocean.

CHAPTER 11

THE BAYOU BELLE

Samburu and Fulani jumped onto the deck of Captain Bishop's ship. Both of them noticed that there was something very strange about the ship. It was seemingly unmanned. At the same time they noticed that the *Carolina Gold* slowly began to move toward the mouth of the harbor behind them.

Captain Bishop was the last to jump onto the deck. "Well, Your Highness, welcome to the Bayou Belle. She ain't much, but she's paid for," he snickered.

Disinterested in what Captain Bishop was saying, Fulani was horrified that the Carolina Gold was floating away.

"Why is that ship moving? Stop that ship at once! Samburu, tell him to stop that ship at once!" Fulani shouted desperately.

Samburu and Captain Bishop stared at one another with scowls on their faces. After as few moments of a token stand off, both men broke out into hysterical laughter.

Fulani was furious, as she gazed at both men confused.

"Sister, why would I do that? It was my idea for Bambara and his ridiculous Mortisi to come here, was it not? We didn't come here to pick up my cargo. Bambara and his Mortisi were the cargo! I guess now, they *are* the cargo," he chuckled.

"You don't think I saw the way you looked at him and the way father protects him. Even my very own Ashanti warriors flocked to him and promised their lives... THEIR LIVES, to him after only five months! So, how in Nyame's name do you think that makes me feel? I am the true prince of the Ashanti! I am the son of the great Chief Yoruba! Not that displaced runaway Mandinkan! I am!" he yelled emphatically.

Captain Bishop slowly backed away from Samburu. Fulani dropped slowly to the deck with one hand over her mouth and the other on her stomach. She felt as if she was going to be sick and die all at once. Her shame was so great that she struggled to breathe. Fulani lifted her head slowly and looked at Samburu with tears streaming down her face, brokenhearted.

"No brother, you are wrong! You are no prince of the Ashanti. You are the prince of nothing now. You have sold your own people to the invaders! You have sold your soul, brother... your soul!"

"Not so fast, little lady! I believe that you and I have some important business to discuss," interrupted Captain Bishop.

Fulani stood and turned toward the sound of Captain Bishop's voice unable to understand what the captain was yelling to her. At that moment Ibos warriors began to climb over both sides of the ship behind her.

Samburu turned aggressively toward Captain Bishop.

"My sister has no part in our arrangement, Captain! I warn you, if one hair on her head is touched... my father's wrath will be swift, I assure you!"

Captain Bishop slowly pulled his cutlass from its scabbard. The smile slowly left his face and was replaced by a determined scowl.

"Oh, I beg to differ, your cry-ness!"

Captain Bishop moved quickly toward Samburu and Fulani. Samburu turned to his sister.

"Run, Fulani! Run!"

The captain plunged his blade deep into Samburu's back. Samburu's eyes widened as he looked down and saw the four inch blade of the cutlass protruding from his chest.

Fulani looked on in horror and then turned to escape only to see multiple Ibos warriors climbing over the bulwark of the ship.

Captain Bishop yanked his cutlass out of Samburu's body and spun away. Samburu fell to the deck with a lifeless thud.

Fulani bent down and stroked her brother's head gently with her right hand. "May Nyame the Omnipotent take pity on your soul, brother."

The bald Ibos warrior from Bambara's story jumped down onto the deck last. He and his warriors surrounded Fulani as she knelt by her brother's corpse. Captain Bishop called upon the leader of the Ibos.

"Anlo!"

The bald Ibos warrior responded and looked over at the captain.

"I do not want her injured in any way. Do you understand?"

Anlo nodded to him, then grabbed a belaying pin from the bulwark. The other Ibos grabbed belaying pins as well. Anlo pointed to five of his warriors and signaled them to move in on Fulani. The five warriors encircled her and began to move in slowly. Fulani closed her eyes and breathed deeply. She opened them and watched the five approaching warriors. Captain Bishop looked on in anticipation, smiling.

Fulani pulled her sickle knives fast and spun through the oncoming warriors, striking each one as she passed. All anyone could hear was the clanking of weapons colliding. Fulani stopped on the other side of the warriors with her back to them and their backs to her. She shook the blood off her sickle knives with one quick jerk of her arms. The blood that hit the deck sounded as if someone had poured water from a cup onto it. She raised her head and stared menacingly at Captain Bishop as the first five Ibos warriors fell simultaneously to the deck— dead.

Fulani twirled her sickle knives stylishly and returned them to their harnesses behind her head.

The other Ibos looked at each other unsure. Without warning, Fulani swiftly removed the bow from her back and began to shoot arrows at the Ibos warriors. She shot an arrow and hit an Ibos warrior in the forehead. He was flipped backwards into the water. She immediately pulled another arrow and shot. An Ibos warrior took the arrow in the chest and dropped where he stood.

She ran, dove in the air and shot another arrow, hitting yet another Ibos warrior in his genitals. The warrior grabbed the arrow with both hands and fell to the deck moaning in agonizing pain. Fulani hit the deck, rolled over and jumped to her feet. She threw her bow down and once again pulled her sickle knives from behind her head.

Anlo, the leader of the Ibos looked down at his dead and wounded warriors strewn on the deck in front of the defiant Fulani. He raised his hand to chest level instructing the rest of his warriors to stay back. Anlo walked calmly over to one of his remaining warriors and snatched a war club from him. He patted the business end of the club into the palm of his left hand as he turned to face Fulani who was watching his every move as she stood at the ready waiting for their next attack.

Anlo walked confidently towards Fulani, stepping over his dead as he did so. Fulani took a deep breath, then attempted to walk toward Anlo, but before she took her first step in his direction, she heard the distinctive click of a pistol hammer being cocked.

Fulani slowly turned her head to the left, slightly, and saw Captain Bishop with a flintlock pistol to the back of her head. She sighed and hung her head before reluctantly dropping her sickle knives to the deck. Captain Bishop addressed Fulani in a calm and smooth tone.

"Darling, don't be sad. This is just the beginning of a long and fruitful relationship for you and I." He smiled then turned his head slightly to give an order to the Ibos.

Blindingly fast, Fulani grabbed Captain Bishop's arm and hand. She pushed his arm and pistol in the direction of Anlo and placed her finger over Captain Bishop's on the trigger, then forced the captain to discharge his weapon. Anlo was hit directly between the eyes. His eyes went crossed and a perfectly circular wound was left, as blood trickled from it. He fell to the deck limp and lifeless.

Captain Bishop pulled his arm free and struck Fulani in the face with his pistol, knocking her unconscious. She fell to the deck motionless. The captain turned to his men and barked out his orders.

"Get her secured below! We set sail for South Carolina at first light! I want all hands on deck! Tell them boys to break camp and get their asses back to this boat," he pointed to the dead bodies on his deck and continued. "Secondly, throw this fish food over the side!"

Anlo, along with all the other dead warriors, were lifted up by the remaining Ibos warriors and unceremoniously thrown over the side of the ship, where their bodies disappeared into the deep.

CHAPTER 12

MORTISI RISE

On the deck of the *Carolina Gold*, Captain Fletcher stood at the helm with both hands on the ship's wheel. The four crewmen raised the anchor until it stopped. Each of them left the cathead and walked behind the captain and knelt to conceal themselves. The crewman closest to Captain Fletcher kept his eyes trained on the captain in anticipation of a signal. Captain Fletcher turned slightly to the crewman closest to him and nodded.

The crewman lowered his head and scanned the deck immediately in front of him. He reached down and lifted a small section of the deck that revealed multiple hidden muskets and powder horns, which he began to quietly distribute to the other crewmen. One of the other four crewmen looked down at his musket, cocked the hammer slowly then stood.

Bambara and the Mortisi, still intoxicated, lay

on the deck in a deep sleep. Many of them were sleeping so well, that they snored as if they were in their own huts.

The lead crewman made his way to the cargo hold and slowly removed the lock from it quietly so none of the Mortisi would be awakened. A few moments after the lock on the hold was removed, the hold door was slid back carefully by the Ibos warriors who were hiding in the belly of the ship. Each of them was armed with their deadly war clubs. One by one, 15 Ibos warriors stealthily exited the hold and took positions around the sleeping Mortisi.

Simon, the fiddler, pretended to be asleep on the deck near Bambara and the beautiful dancing girl. He watched from the corner of his eye as the Ibos positioned themselves.

Once all of them were in position, they began to implement their plan. Two Ibos warriors stood over one of the sleeping Mortisi furthest from the others. Simultaneously the Ibos placed a knotted gag into the sleeping Mortisi's mouth as the other threw shackles upon his wrists.

The Mortisi warrior, still groggy from the effects of the opium, struggled to no avail.

Another Ibos swung his war club striking the Mortisi in the head, knocking him unconscious immediately. Then with one synchronized move, they lifted his body and carried him silently down into the cargo hold.

Simon, witnessing what was happening, attempted to wake Bambara without causing any attention to himself.

"Hey! Heeeey! Pssst! Hey! Waaake uuup," he whispered.

Bambara tossed and mumbled a little, but did not awaken. Simultaneously, some Ibos warriors gagged, shackled and knocked unconscious another of the Mortisi, then quickly scurried him into the dark of the cargo hold.

Captain Fletcher pointed to the Ibos warrior nearest the sleeping Bambara. He signaled to him that he wanted Bambara to be the next Mortisi carried to the hold. Three of the largest Ibos began to move cautiously towards Bambara. One pulled the knotted gag tightly between his hands. The other held shackles at the ready and the last held a war club with dried blood on the tip from previous use. The Ibos warrior holding the gag grinned confidently as he prepared to pounce on Bambara.

Simon, still pretending to be asleep saw the Ibos preparing to kidnap Bambara as they had done to many others before him. Suddenly, Simon sat up turned his head in the direction of Bambara and fake sneezed as loud as he could muster. Bambara's eyes opened immediately.

The startled Ibos warriors took their eyes off of Bambara and looked over at Simon in disbelief. Bambara saw the shackles in the second Ibos' hands. He yelled like a madman, as he up-kicked the Ibos with the shackles in the face, knocking him backwards.

The one holding the war club immediately stood straight and raised the club over his head preparing to deal a blow to Bambara, but he grabbed the Ibos with the knotted gag by the back of the head and pulled him forward to the deck on top of him. He lifted both his legs backwards and placed the head of the Ibos warrior with the gag between his knees. He jerked sharply at the waist and snapped the neck of the Ibos who was holding the gag. The warrior's body went limp.

Captain Fletcher looked on with concern but

did not move from his position at the helm.

The Ibos warrior holding the war club over his head brought it down trying to hit Bambara. Bambara rolled out of the way of the oncoming blow, then, up-kipped to his feet. He searched the immediate area around him for some kind of weapon. All he could find was a pouch of arrows with no bow. He cried out desperately for his comrades.

"Mortisi rise! We are under attack! Mortisi rise!"

The remaining Mortisi warriors on the deck finally awoke and jumped up to find themselves surrounded by Ibos warriors. Still feeling the effects of the drugs and drink, they looked at one another confused before attacking the Ibos with reckless abandon, some with their bare hands.

Captain Fletcher stomped his heel on the deck. Suddenly, many white crewmen ran up from the cargo hold carrying muskets. They quickly lined up in front of Captain Fletcher and stood at the ready, as they faced the melee.

Bambara picked up a knotted gag from the deck. He took it in both hands and pulled it tight between them.

The Ibos with the war club and the one with the shackles moved around him cautiously as they stalked him. The Ibos warrior with the war club swung it at Bambara as if trying to swat a hive of bees from a tree. Each time he swung the club, Bambara could hear it cut through the wind. Bambara skillfully blocked the club a couple of times with the gag. The Ibos continued to swing the club wildly at him.

On his next attack the Ibos swung his club recklessly. Bambara blocked the club with the gag and wrapped it around the tip of the war club. He used leverage as he twisted his body and the gag simultaneously and flipped the Ibos warrior over on his back onto the deck. Without hesitation Bambara reached down, grabbed the war club from the stunned Ibos warrior's hand and raised it over his own head as high as he could. Then he brought it down into the warrior's face with intense rage, with all of his might, bashing the warrior's head in. Brain matter and bits of skull splattered onto the deck.

The Ibos warrior holding the shackles charged towards Bambara as he swung the shackles over his head. Bambara barely managed to elude the heavy iron shackles being swung at his head. He spun and swung the war club at the same time, striking the Ibos warrior with a mighty blow to the jaw, knocking his lower jawbone away from the rest of his face. The warrior stopped advancing immediately and fell face first to the deck.

Bambara craned his head to the left, then to the right in anticipation of another attack. Once he realized no attacks were imminent, he looked up at Captain Fletcher on the helm. He glared at him as he placed the war club under his arm and put both his pointer fingers into his mouth and whistled.

The remaining Mortisi stopped fighting where they stood and scurried quickly to Bambara's side. They were breathing hard and covered in Ibos' blood.

Captain Fletcher stared down at Bambara and the rest of the Mortisi from his vantage point behind his line of armed crewmen and nonchalantly applauded.

"Most impressive, but I'm afraid this dance is over!"

Bambara turned his head and glanced into

each of the faces of his remaining Mortisi.

"It has been my life's honor to lead you, brothers! Now, I give you one final command!"

He turned defiantly and faced Captain Fletcher and his men once more. Each one of the ship's armed crewmen trained his musket on one of the remaining Mortisi.

Bambara, realizing neither he nor his men would survive the next assault, thought of his mother, Fulani, and his beloved village at the same time. He closed his eyes and prayed under his breath. "May Nyame welcome me to His table."

He opened his eyes with a determined look upon his face.

"The Mortisi will never be slaves! Fiiiiight!"

Bambara lifted the war club in his right hand toward the smug Captain Fletcher. Suddenly, he charged towards them, jumping over the bodies of the fallen. The Mortisi followed closely behind yelling like men possessed.

One Mortisi warrior notched an arrow in his bow as he attacked. He loosed the arrow and hit one of the crewmen in the stomach. The crewman dropped his musket and grabbed the arrow lodged in his abdomen as he fell.

Another of the crewmen discharged his musket. The Mortisi warrior who had shot the arrow was hit in the throat. He grabbed his neck and fell to the deck. Three crewmen positioned in the cargo hold fired on the Mortisi simultaneously. Two Mortisi to Bambara's left were hit and tumbled to the deck. All three of the crewmen in the hold attempted to reload rapidly.

One of the Mortisi warriors diverted his charge and ran toward the three men in the hold. He pulled an arrow from the pouch under his arm and dove as he war cried into the crewmen. All four men tumbled into the hold. As they all hit bottom, the Mortisi warrior rolled to his right and stabbed one of the men in the throat with the tip of his arrow. He swiftly rolled back to his left and lost in rage, stabbed another of the men in the stomach.

The third crewmen quickly moved away from the others and jumped to his feet. He pulled his cutlass, then ran up behind and chopped the Mortisi warrior in the back, causing a gaping wound. The Mortisi yelled in pain but continued to stab the second crewmen with the arrow repeatedly.

The third crewmen, in awe of the Mortisi warrior's strength, attempted to help his fellow crewman and began stabbing him until he stopped poking the already dead crewmen. After being punctured by the cutlass several times, the Mortisi warrior finally turned and fell to the floor bleeding from his mouth and stomach profusely. His breathing labored and the blood in his lungs gurgled as he looked up at the third crewman then coughed up blood.

"I am still free, Barbarian. May Nyame welcome me," he declared defiantly before dying with his eyes trained on the remaining crewmen.

Bambara switched the war club to his left hand and picked up a pike lying on top of the lifeless body of one of the fallen Ibos warriors. He stood straight again, picked his target and threw the pike as hard as he could. The pike hit a crewman who was standing closely behind Captain Fletcher. The force of the pike lifted him off of his feet and knocked him into the rail. Captain Fletcher did not waver in the least as he stood at the helm confidently.

Bambara and his eight remaining Mortisi fought their way to within only a few feet from the captain before he pulled two custom shotgun style pistols from the thick leather holsters he wore on both his hips. He lifted them up in each of his hands and trained them on the charging Mortisi. Bambara was in the center of his men as they all charged fearlessly. Captain Fletcher fired the shotgun pistol in his left hand.

Five of the remaining Mortisi warriors to the right of Bambara were hit by hundreds of tiny lead balls from the shotgun shells inside of the captain's weapon. Two warriors grabbed their faces, two others were hit in the chest and one was hit in the head and fell to the deck instantly.

Bambara and the last of his men continued to charge valiantly. Captain Fletcher smiled as he discharged the weapon in his right hand and wiped out the last of the Mortisi. Bambara too was hit. He staggered, determined to kill Captain Fletcher with the war club raised above his head, before he lost consciousness and fell to the deck with a bloody wound on the side of his forehead.

CHAPTER 13

I AM A STUDENT OF HISTORY

The next time Bambara's eyes opened he was in the dank and dreary confines of the cargo hold of the *Carolina Gold*. It was an experience with which he was all too familiar. He shivered uncontrollably on the floor and tried to warm himself by wrapping both his arms as tightly as he could around his torso and balling himself into the fetal position. His eyes were swollen, sealed shut by his own dried blood and he was sweating feverishly.

The sound of a whip cracking and screams of excruciating agony pierced the night and Bambara quickly lifted his head off the floor to try to determine if it was one of his Mortisi who was being tortured. He moved his right leg and heard the chain connected to his shackles rattle. Dejected, he slowly laid his head down on the floor once again.

On the deck of the *Carolina Gold* heavy rains

pelted the deck, as well as the men standing on it. Gale force winds whistled and slammed huge waves into the hull of the ship.

Simon, the well-intentioned fiddler, was secured to the main mast. His arms were chained above his head with his back against the mast. The fiddler's white frilly shirt with the fancy sleeves was now a bloody rag. It was ripped and oozing blood from where he had been beaten across the stomach and chest with the whip. He had trouble keeping his eyes open with the force of the rain droplets stinging his face. He looked up at Mr. Collins, the man responsible for carrying out the captain's punishment on Simon. Four crewmen looked on as Mr. Collins carried out the sordid act.

Simon whimpered as he pleaded. "Please, Mr. Collins, no more, Please!"

Mr. Collins, a medium built man, was thin with a scraggly beard. He continued to strike Simon's body, ignoring his plea. Mr. Collins yelled at Simon angrily.

"You took the side of those monkeys over us, you little bastard! A lot of our boys died because of you tonight! The captain doesn't want me to but we all want to kill your ass! Lucky for you I am a man who follows his captain's orders. So, I'll just wait. But the time will come. You and I will settle this thing!"

Mr. Collins began to wrap the whip up in his hand and turned his back. Simon, thankful and weak, raised his head to the sky and proclaimed, "Thank you God! Thank you God!" relieved that his punishment was over.

Mr. Collins slowly turned back towards Simon and smirked sinisterly as he allowed the whip to unroll to the deck once more. Simon lowered his head and looked at the whip in Mr. Collin's hand.

"Well, I can't kill you, but I can leave you with something to remember me by!"

Mr. Collins swung the whip with all of his might. Simon screamed in agony as the whip tore across his body. Mr. Collins cracked his whip again. Again, Simon hollered in pain. Mr. Collins cracked the whip once more and smiled as he wrapped the bloody whip into a tight circle in his hands.

Simon's body went limp as he hung on the mast unconscious. Upon his face were three skull deep scars from where Mr. Collins had struck him. Mr. Collins turned his head towards two of the crewmen who where watching and ordered, "Get him cleaned up, then take him to the captain!"

Captain Fletcher was seated in an ornate, high back, wooden chair in his cabin. He wore a gold pair of spectacles at the tip of his nose as he flipped through the pages of a book. The shelves surrounding him were full of books and there was a large map of the entire continent of Africa resting in the center of a large table in the center of the room. Suddenly, there was a knock at his cabin door. The captain stopped reading and lifted his head.

"Come in!" he shouted toward the door.

The two crewmen who Mr. Collins had ordered to bring Simon to the captain entered his quarters dragging the wounded boy. Each man had one hand under each of Simon's armpits. His feet dragged limply along the floor. Bloodstained rudimentary bandages covered his face and head. Only his right eye was left uncovered.

The crewmen dragged him to the front of

Captain Fletcher's desk and dropped him onto all fours. Simon stayed on his hands and knees for a brief moment then struggled to get to his feet. He turned his head slightly to the left and peered at the captain with his right eye from beneath his bandages.

Captain Fletcher remained seated and seemed unconcerned about the presence of the battered Simon. He addressed Simon as if he was a professor teaching a class.

"I am a student of history, Did you know that about me, Simon? Do you like history?"

Simon was unresponsive.

The captain continued.

"You can find so many answers to the problems we face in our own time in the pages of antiquity. Take, for instance, the Romans. If a Roman soldier betrayed his commanding officer he was dismembered in front of all the members of his regiment. They did this to discourage any future attempt to disobey orders."

Captain Fletcher closed the book he was reading and removed his glasses. He placed both the book and glasses onto a small table beside his chair. He stood, placing his hands behind his back as he walked toward Simon.

"What do you think I should do with you? You've disappointed me terribly, Simon. You're an educated and cultured young man and I find your violin playing exquisite. As a matter of fact, the only reason you are still alive is that you are my indentured servant. Your father still owes me quite a large sum of money. Unfortunately for you, your father is not the best card player in the world. If he were, you wouldn't be in this predicament in the first place, would you?"

The captain turned to the crewmen and laughed hysterically. He turned back and bent at the knees until he was face-to-face with Simon. Captain Fletcher slowly lifted Simon's bandage to the side a little and looked at the deep wounds to Simon's face.

"What a pity, you were such a handsome lad. Well, looks like those days are over. You will heal soon enough but I do believe the days of the finest ladies in the South waiting in line for violin lessons are over!"

Simon hung his head sadly.

Captain Fletcher giggled, then pulled the bandage back over Simon's scar, stood and turned his back on him.

"Well, your new responsibilities will not be as cosmopolitan as you have been used to. Your new duties will be one befitting a traitorous leech, such as yourself. You will now slop the pigs in the cargo hold."

Simon looked up at Captain Fletcher confused.

"You want me to slop the pigs, sir?"

Captain Fletcher smiled at Simon.

"Yes, I want you to slop the pigs. Take care of the animals. I want you to feed the slaves, boy! We will not be able to fetch a good price at market if they look sickly, will we? So starting tomorrow morning, that will be your new job-- taking care of the livestock. Oh, there is one other thing. Disobey my orders again and I will be sending your ass back to your degenerate gambling father... in five different crates!"

Simon hung his head solemnly once more.

Captain Fletcher looked at Simon disgusted. He turned to the crewmen.

"Now, get him out of my sight!"

The two crewmen grabbed Simon under his armpits and took him out of the captain's cabin.

CHAPTER 14

INSTRUMENT OF MY REVENGE

Bambara could not easily keep track of time because his stomach was churning so much from the constant swaying and dipping of the ship in which he was imprisoned. The swelling in his eyes had subsided enough to see the whites of them again. He sat with his back against the wall, chained, as he sat on the cold, damp floor with his knees up and his elbows resting on them.

Suddenly, the cargo hold door slid back and the bright sunrays penetrated the bleak darkness of the malodorous hold. Bambara and the other prisoners in the hold blocked the sun with their arms and hands to prevent its rays from hitting their eyes, which were tremendously light sensitive.

Simon climbed down the ladder to the floor of the hold. He carried a wooden bucket in his left hand. His face was still bandaged. Simon removed a large wooden spoon out of the bucket and began to feed the prisoners. He dumped a liberal amount of gruel made from wild oats, cornmeal and discarded bits of slop from the galley into the pleading hands of the starving captives.

Simon had served several of the prisoners before turning his head and seeing Bambara. Bambara sat motionless as he watched Simon feed the other captives. Slowly, Simon made his way back to Bambara. He apprehensively placed the spoon back into the bucket and pulled out a large portion of the gruel.

Bambara stared right through Simon, cold and emotionless. Swiftly, he kicked his right leg up and knocked the entire contents of the spoon all over Simon.

Simon quickly dropped the bucket to the floor. He shook and wiped the food remnants off the front of his shirt and pants, then sighed. He looked up from the mess that Bambara created and spoke to him slowly and deliberately to help him understand his words.

"If you do not eat, big fellow, you will never be able to survive this journey."

Bambara looked at Simon with murder on his mind. He turned away from Simon.

"We are going to have to learn to communicate, you and I. What... is... your.... name?"

Simon pointed to himself. "I... am... Si-mon."

Simon pointed to Bambara. "You... are?"

Bambara tried to ignore this colorless barbarian, but became curious and turned back toward Simon. After Simon repeated his name, Bambara decided to try to learn as much as he could about these strange people from across the great river.

Simon pointed to Bambara once more.

"You are?"

Bambara pointed to himself, mimicking Simon. Simon nearly burst with excitement when he saw that Bambara was trying to communicate with him. He pointed to himself.

"I... am... Si-mon."

Simon pointed back to Bambara.

"You... are?"

Bambara pointed to himself.

"Bam... bara. Bambara."

Simon could not believe it. He looked into

Bambara's face ecstatically.

"Your name is Bambara? That is your name... Bambara."

Bambara nodded to Simon before lying down on the floor. Simon stood and looked down at Bambara.

"Big fellow, you and I are going to become friends whether you want to or not. For you will be the instrument of my revenge," he said sinisterly, before reaching up to his face and gently touching the bandages wrapped around his head.

"Sleep well my large friend. Tomorrow we will begin your schooling."

Captain Fletcher and Mr. Collins stood in the center of the captain's quarters studying charts on the table.

"We have to make sure we use all available space in the hold. I don't want to sail all the way back to Georgia with a half-filled hold. How many days do you estimate until we make Sierra Leone?" inquired the captain.

Mr. Collins began to answer confidently. "I estimate..." Mr. Collins was interrupted mid-sentence by a soft knock at the door.

Captain Fletcher lifted his head quickly and yelled toward the door.

"Come in!"

Simon entered the cabin. He walked through the threshold carrying a book. Simon cowered, lowering his head as to not make any eye contact with either man.

Mr. Collins smirked as Captain Fletcher intentionally startled Simon.

"What do you want, boy? I'm busy here!"

Simon responded immediately, but stammered.

"I'm t... te... terribly sorry to bother you, sir. But, I would like to..."

Captain Fletcher grew impatient. "For God's sake man, spit it out!"

Simon tried his best to keep himself steady.

"I would like to return this book you lent me a while ago."

Captain Fletcher waved his hand at Simon dismissively and returned his gaze down to the map again.

Mr. Collins smiled at Simon.

"How's the face?" he asked mockingly.

The captain laughed while continuing to

study his charts.

Simon gritted his teeth and glared at Mr. Collins, seething. He slowly turned and walked over to one of the bookshelves. He placed the book back into the only open space left on the shelf.

Mr. Collins slowly turned back to the map as well.

Simon turned his head slightly and peeped over at the captain and Mr. Collins. Seeing that the two of them were no longer paying any attention to him, he quickly grabbed a large leather bound book from the shelf and placed it in the front of his pants before he turned and headed for the door. He could hear his heart beating rapidly as he reached out for the doorknob.

Just before Simon could make his escape, Mr. Collins lifted his head.

"You never answered my question, boy!" he hollered forcefully, as he stared at Simon from the table awaiting his response.

Simon turned his head nervously. Though he wanted to let his anger out in a deluge of vim, Simon composed himself before answering.

"It's healing, Mr. Collins."

Mr. Collins scoffed.

"Glad to hear it. Now get out of here, Traitor!"

Simon yanked the door open and left as fast as he could. He shut the door behind him and paused outside of it, trying to slow down his breathing. He was excited and had an adrenaline rush from his heist but all Simon could hear was Mr. Collins' laughter echoing in his head-- *"How's the face? How's the face? How's the face?"*

Simon pulled the book he had stolen from the front of his pants and glanced down at it. He ran his fingers over the beautifully bound book's title-- THE HISTORY OF EGYPT, positioned directly above a picture of a large, black ankh. Both were elegantly embossed into the faded leather cover.

Suddenly, Simon could hear a couple of crewmen headed in his direction. He frantically placed the book back into his pants and walked past the crewmen with his head down.

CHAPTER 15

THE ENEMY OF MY ENEMY

Bambara sat with his back against the wall, dejected and weak. *"What have I done in my young life to deserve such a punishment from Nyame?"* he asked himself.

The hold was full of Africans bound for slavery in the Americas. All that filled his ears were women and men sobbing and a morbid symphony of sickly coughs. Bambara felt as if he would go mad. Hearing the sound of the cargo hold door sliding back, he wearily raised his head and saw Simon climbing down the ladder with a slop bucket.

Once he got to the bottom, Simon turned and began to parcel out the gruel from the bucket to the host of chained Africans, who begged and pleaded, with their hands outstretched, for a mouthful of nourishment.

He dipped the large wooden spoon into the bucket and began to dole out food into their eager hands. Simon slowly moved toward where Bambara was chained. Once close, he bent at the knees and squatted in front of Bambara.

Bambara frowned at him suspiciously.

"How are you today big fellow? Are we going to eat today... or will I be wearing your dinner once more?" Simon said jokingly. He smiled for a moment then became serious.

Scowling suspiciously, Bambara continued to glare at Simon. Simon moved slowly and deliberately as he removed the spoon from the bucket. He cautiously moved the spoon towards Bambara. Bambara lifted his hands swiftly toward Simon. Simon flinched instantly in anticipation of Bambara smacking the food out of his hands. To his amazement, Bambara raised his pointer finger on his right hand from a fist and pointed to Simon non-threateningly, as he spoke to him in a thick African accent.

"I Si...mon."

Simon's eyes widened with amazement.

"Holy shit! You are a smart one, aren't you? That is very good!"

Simon pointed to himself. "I am Simon."

Simon pointed at Bambara. "You are

Bambara."

Bambara recognized his name and nodded his head in approval. Simon looked up at the cargo hold door to make sure no one was watching them. He then reached into the front of his pants and pulled the book he had stolen from Captain Fletcher's quarters out and showed it to Bambara.

Bambara studied the book quizzically.

"I am going to teach you to read. You don't know what I am saying to you now, but you will with a little effort and a whole lot of luck, my friend."

At that moment a crewman began to climb down the ladder into the hold. A bullwhip hung from his belt rolled up.

Simon quickly placed the book back into his pants, then paused for a moment and thought. Simon gave Bambara a wink before he stood and poured the remainder of the contents in the bucket onto the front of his clothes.

"Goddamnit! You black bastard! Look what you've done! That's it, you son of a bitch! There will be no more food for you for a long damn time!" Simon yelled, as he stood pointing down at Bambara.

Bambara scowled at Simon thinking to himself that these colorless barbarians are out of their minds. He could not understand why Simon poured food on himself and yelled at him.

The crewman ran over to Simon. "What's this buck doin'? I'll take the whip to his mangy hide!" threatened the crewman.

Simon shook the food off the front of his shirt. The crewman pulled the whip from the front of his pants and let it unfurl onto the damp, urine soaked floor and prepared to strike Bambara.

Bambara stared up at the crewman defiantly.

The crewman pulled his right arm back as far as he could. Just before his arm came forward Simon grabbed the crewman's arm. He spoke to him in a calm manner.

"Whipping this nigger is not good enough. We should separate his troublesome ass from these others before they get the same ideas, don't you think?"

The crewman dropped the hand with the whip to his side and thought.

"I know! We'll put this nigger in the pen over

there by himself. That'll teach his black ass who's in charge!"

"Oh, that sounds like a splendid idea!" Simon concurred and smiled slyly. "That is an excellent idea, my friend!"

The crewman pulled the keys to unlock the chains from his pocket. He bent over and unlocked the section of chain that was holding Bambara to the floor. Then he escorted Bambara over to a 3 x 4 foot pen, down a dark hall, which was about thirty feet from the other captive Africans. Once at the entrance of the pen, the crewman pushed Bambara violently into the pen. Bambara turned aggressively toward the crewman, but refrained from retaliating.

The crewman grabbed Bambara's shackled hands and chained him to a steel ring hanging on the wall, then took a few steps back as he unwrapped the bullwhip.

Simon saw the crewman preparing to whip Bambara and quickly intervened.

"If you wouldn't mind, I'm the one wearing this nigger's dinner. If you would be so kind as to allow me." Simon held out his hand for the whip.

The crewman smiled dubiously and handed the whip to Simon.

"And make sure you whip this one good. He is much too proud! Pride is no good for a nigga! He gotta be broke before he can be sold at auction." the crewman taunted and kicked at Bambara.

"Don't you worry about that! I'm going to beat him within inches of his miserable, Godforsaken life! Of that you can be sure!"

The crewman laughed hysterically and left.

Simon laid the end of the whip onto the floor and motioned to Bambara with his hands, attempting to encourage him to react. He cracked the whip against the wall.

Bambara cringed, then opened his eyes when he did not feel the sting of the lash on his flesh. Confused, he sat there and watched Simon in silence.

The crewman at the ladder stopped and turned his head slightly to listen the screams of agony from Bambara. Simon cracked the whip against the wall once more.

The crewman shook his head in disappointment and began to walk back to the pen.

Simon looked at Bambara and implored him to yell, scream, or do anything, as if he was in pain.

Bambara looked up at Simon, finally figuring out what he was asking him to do.

Simon cracked the whip again against the wall.

Bambara yelled as if he was in intense pain.

The crewman heard Bambara yell. He giggled and shook his head again as he turned back around and headed away from the pen.

Simon continued to crack the whip against the wall, as Bambara simultaneously faked being in pain. He and Simon looked at one another and smiled as they continued their charade through the night.

CHAPTER 16

I WILL BE CALLED RAMSES

The next day Simon returned to Bambara's pen with the book in hand. He looked down at Bambara seated on the floor.

"Now it is time to teach you to read, my large friend."

Bambara looked up at his new friend quizzically. Simon, careful not to make any movements that could have been construed as threatening, slowly took a seat on the moist floor beside him. He opened the book to the first page and began to read aloud.

Bambara did not understand the words, but he did understand the importance of learning the language of his enemy. So he sat there listening to the sounds coming from Simon's mouth.

On rainy days, Simon and Bambara would sit on the soaking wet floor holding a ratty blanket over their heads to protect the book from the rainwater that poured through the deck of the ship. Bambara held a small candle over the book so he and Simon could see what they were reading.

After two months of reading the book to Bambara, the day had finally come for the Mandinka to read for himself. He pointed to each word on the page as he read from the book in a thick African accent. Simon looked on quite pleased with his efforts, as he watched his pupil read for the first time. Bambara only struggled with a few words. When he did, Simon would quickly say and explain the meaning of the word until Bambara would nod that he understood. Then, Bambara took the book once more from Simon and continued to read.

Simon knew that no matter what propaganda was being spread about blacks, being less than human in the Americas, was a terrible lie.

~

The next night the ship was caught in the eye of a violent storm. It rocked and swayed on the huge swells.

Bambara sat in the pen reading. He was at the end of the book. Concentrating on the last pages, he suddenly heard someone trying to remove the chain from the door of the pen. Quickly, he put the book under some of the hay that was strewn on the floor of the pen behind him and looked up at the door. He was relieved when Simon walked into the pen.

Simon stepped into the pen and pulled two large red apples from under his water drenched raincoat and handed them to Bambara.

"Have you finished the book?" he asked with jovial anticipation.

Bambara grinned at Simon before he reached back and grabbed the book from under the hay. He brushed the hay off the cover and handed it to Simon, then crawled over to a small section of floor and removed a small piece of board where he had a secret food stash. Bambara placed the apples inside and covered them with the piece of board again before responding to Simon's query in his strong African accent.

"Yes, I finish book. I understand da words now. Tank you, my friend. How long fore we reach where they take I?"

Simon impressed, answered, "Well now! Haven't you become quite the orator? We arrive in Carolina in the next couple of days."

Bambara was saddened by the news and hung his head.

Simon walked over to Bambara and took a seat next to him. "Tell me, what was your absalute favorite thing in the book?"

Bambara looked up at the ceiling and thought hard. "Warrior king, Ramses. He ruled his people like true king should. Simon, I tank you for teach me to read. When great Nyame give me chance for revenge, I promise I kill you last."

Simon started to thank him, then, realized what Bambara had said.

Bambara grinned jokingly at Simon.

Simon stood and turned back to Bambara.

"Don't mention it my friend. I would like to ask a favor of you, if I could?"

Simon began to unwrap the bandages around his face.

"Yes, what is this favor?"

Simon's bandages fell to the floor at the feet of Bambara.

"Do not call me Simon anymore. I would like to be called... he thought hard... Scars. Yes, I rather like the sound of it. Scars!"

Bambara slowly raised his head and looked

into his friend's face. What he saw was horrible. Simon's face had deep, grotesque horizontal gashes left across his face by Mr. Collins' beating of him.

Bambara could not help but stare at his friend's face. He nodded and smiled.

"Scars? I like dis name. I too wish to be called by another name from this night on... I will be called Ramses! Like da king in da book! Bambara died when 'dey took my Fulani and my freedom a second time. I will find her again, as well as my freedom, to dis I swear on all da gods!"

Lightning flashed and thunder cracked in the sky as Ramses stood and looked into Scars' face, then lifted his shackled wrists to him. Scars looked down at the shackles and nodded.

CHAPTER 17

THE STORM

On the deck of the Carolina Gold that same night, the storm raged. Captain Fletcher stood on the bow and watched helplessly as giant wave after giant wave crashed against his beloved ship. The ship was tossed up and down and side to side like a kid's toy on the angry seas. Winds howled as huge drops of stinging rain pelted him in the face. The captain turned and ran towards the helm where a crewman struggled to hold onto the ship's wheel.

Mr. Collins hurried over to Captain Fletcher with concern.

"It's a bad one, captain and I believe the eye is headed straight for us, sir!" he yelled

Captain Fletcher shouted his reply.

"I want all of the hatches battened down and the sails pulled immediately to keep us from capsizing!"

The captain pushed the crewman on the ship's

wheel away rudely and grabbed it himself. He could feel the rudder being bashed in the heavy swells as he wrestled with the wheel, struggling to keep the ship on course.

The crewmen on deck struggled to get the sails down from the main mast as wind gusts filled them, making them nearly impossible to lower.

Scars watched as the crewman with the keys to the chains carefully came down the ladder into the hold. He reached the bottom and looked around the hold. The crewman stopped when he saw the young teenage African girl he had been keeping his eye on. He grabbed the chain she was connected to and opened the lock with the key, then pulled the chains that were connected to the shackles on her tiny wrists.

"Come here, bitch!" he commanded disrespectfully.

The girl tried her best to resist, but to no avail. He pulled her into a dark corner of the filthy hold and began to pull his pants down. The terrified child cringed into the corner because she knew what the crewman's intentions were. But her eyes widened when she saw Scars creeping up behind the crewman holding a boarding axe in his hands.

The crewman seeing the expression on the young girl's face, smiled. "Never seen one this big before, huh girly?" he asked then chuckled proudly.

At that very moment Scars buried the axe into the back of the crewman's skull with a dull thud. The African girl trembled with fear as the crewman slowly turned and faced Scars standing behind him. The crewman took an aggressive step toward Scars before his eyes rolled up into his head and he fell face first to the floor with his pants around his knees.

Scars quickly lifted his pointer finger to his mouth.

"Shhhhhhhh."

He bent over and removed the key ring from the dead crewman's belt and ran down the hall, stopping in front of a closed door. Fumbling through the keys he finally located the one to unlock the door. He inserted the key and opened the door to the weapon and ammunition storeroom. Without hesitation he entered the room and began to grab muskets, ammunition, and gunpowder.

Above deck, the ship's constant rocking made the footing treacherous for the crew, as well as hindered their attempt to secure the sails and hatches.

Scars peeked out of the cargo hold door and saw every hand on deck frantically wrestling with the sails to get them down. He turned his head toward the ship's wheel and witnessed Captain Fletcher desperately trying to keep control of the ship's steering.

Suddenly, two crewmen ran by him on their way to assist the other crewmen in securing the sails. Once the men passed, Scars jumped out of the hold with his arms filled with muskets and ammunition. He made his way stealthily over to the longboat closest to the hold and placed the stolen arms into it. He craned his neck to make sure everyone was still occupied before moving toward the other longboats.

Scars pulled a knife from his pocket and started to cut the rope's hold, which held the other longboats to the bulwark, allowing them to fall into the churning, turbulent sea.

Mr. Collins was frantically giving orders and

instructing the men when he inadvertently turned and saw Scars cutting away the longboats. He pivoted to find a crewman to assist him, but could not find one who was not hanging like an acrobat many feet in the air on the main mast.

Scars carried a cutlass on his side tucked into his belt and two muskets over his right shoulder as he crept back into the cargo hold.

Mr. Collins followed him into it soon after. He climbed down the ladder slowly so as not to forewarn Scars before he would have the chance to catch him red-handed.

Dripping with rainwater, Mr. Collins removed the hat from his head and peered into the dimly lit hold. He pulled a one shot pistol from the front of his pants and began to search for Scars. Slowly, he made his way down the hall listening as hard as he could.

Mr. Collins cautiously crossed one foot over the other with his pistol at the ready until he came to the pen where Ramses was being held. Carefully, he entered and saw Ramses chained to the wall, sitting on the floor. The door of the pen slowly creaked then closed behind him.

Without warning, the sound of Scars' cutlass

cut the wind. The arm in which Mr. Collins was holding the pistol was severed at the forearm and fell to the floor in front of him. In shock, he yelled in pain as he grabbed the arm that had been cut and turned, terrified. Mr. Collins saw Scars standing there with a crazed look upon his face and a bloodstained cutlass in his hand.

Mr. Collins backed away from Scars until he bumped into Ramses, who was now standing. Horrified, he turned and saw Ramses holding his freed hands in the air to show he was no longer chained. Mr. Collins turned back to Simon terrified and pleaded.

"Simon! What have you done? I can fix this! Just let me go and I'll fix this right up, boy. I promise!"

Scars turned a deaf ear as he walked toward Mr. Collins slowly.

"You can fix this... huh? You mean like you fixed my face? No, I don't think that will be at all necessary. But, before you go, I would like to give you something to remember me by. Does that sound familiar to you, Mr. Collins?"

Scars raised the cutlass over his head and hacked Mr. Collins down where he stood. Blood splattered into his face and onto the front of his clothing as he hacked Mr. Collins repeatedly with the cutlass, beside himself with rage.

When he finally stopped hacking at the remains, Scars spat on Mr. Collins' body and kicked him in what was left of his face.

Out of breath and covered in blood, he turned to Ramses. "Shall we go?" he asked with a strange calmness.

Ramses looked down at the bloody remains of what was left of Mr. Collins and nodded before running over and grabbing the muskets from behind the pen door. He passed one of the muskets to Scars and the two of them moved quietly through the hall leading to the main cargo hold.

Suddenly, a crewman walked out from a room in the hallway and startled them. Quickly he turned to alert his fellow crewmen, but before he was able to make a sound Ramses rammed the barrel of his musket into his mouth, pulled the trigger and blew the back out of the crewman's head which muffled the shot. The crewman dropped to the floor with the musket barrel lodged in his mouth and smoke wafted from the hole in his head.

Scars sighed silently in relief as he passed Ramses the cutlass before continuing down the hall. Once in the main cargo hold, Ramses looked around at his African brethren chained in the filthy confines of the hold. He lowered his head then turned to Scars.

"We must try ta free 'dem."

Scars glared at Ramses as if he had lost his mind.

"We don't have the time for that!" he whispered.

Ramses glared back at Scars determined.

Scars sighed, then reached into his pocket, pulled out the keys and reluctantly handed the keys to Ramses.

The Africans in the hold lifted their hands desperately and pleaded to be released. Ramses attempted to find the correct keys to the locks, but there were too many and he soon became overwhelmed. Finally becoming too frustrated he just handed the keys to the nearest African man.

"May Nyame bless you all," he spoke in his native tongue.

Ramses walked over to Scars. "Let's we go."

Scars placed his hand onto Ramses' shoulder consolingly and nodded before making their way to the ladder and proceeded to climb out of the hold.

Captain Fletcher struggled to hold the ship on course in the violent waters of the storm. He squinted, attempting to see through the deluge of wind and coin-sized droplets of rain pelting him in the face. The captain wasn't sure of what he saw in front of the ship. So, he wiped the water from his face and peered once more into the gloominess of that night. What he saw sent chills down his spine.

Large dark formations of some kind jutted from the sea bottom in front of the ship, no more than a few hundred yards of their heading. Captain Fletcher wiped his eyes again and concentrated even harder to see through the storm. There was no denying what he saw this time. It was a seafarer's worst nightmare. Exposed pieces of jagged reef towered out of the sea in a direct collision course with the *Carolina Gold.*

Captain Fletcher's eyes widened as he

desperately spun the ship's wheel frantically.

"We're headed for the reef! God help me turn this goddamned wheel!" he yelled desperately.

Two crewmen ran over to the captain to help him veer the ship away from the reef. They grabbed hold of the wheel and turned it with all of their collective strength.

Ramses and Scars climbed out of the hold and crept up behind Captain Fletcher and the two crewmen.

"Good evening, captain!" Scars yelled as he held his musket on the men.

Captain Fletcher and the crewmen released the wheel and turned to face Scars and Bambara. Desperate, Captain Fletcher responded to Scars.

"This is not the time for you to choose the wrong side, boy! This ship is headed directly for that reef out there!"

Ramses and Scars turned to one another in unison. "So what?"

Ramses continued in a furious tone. "Where da other ship take Fulani?"

Captain Fletcher looked at Scars with contempt. "My compliments, Simon. You didn't waste any time these last three months, did you?

You proved you could teach a monkey how to talk. I am going to tell you nothing, nigger!"

Ramses walked toward Captain Fletcher clutching the cutlass. Then, without warning, he slashed both the crewmen who stood to both sides of the captain with his cutlass, lightning fast. The crewmen's heads tumbled from their bodies and hit the deck with dull thuds. Their bodies dropped simultaneously in front of Captain Fletcher. Ramses stepped over their bodies and stood face to face with the captain.

"I will only ask dis once more. Where dey take Fulani?"

Captain Fletcher trembled as he looked down at the headless bodies of his crewmen.

"If I tell you... you'll kill me anyway!"

Ramses looked back at Scars, then turned back to Captain Fletcher.

"If you tell me where they take Fulani, I will not kill you. I swear dis on I honor!"

Scars looked at Ramses in disbelief.

"You what?" Scars screamed angrily.

Captain Fletcher calmed himself after hearing Ramses' promise. He sighed, then spoke.

"Captain Bishop took her to his plantation in

South Carolina. He wants her to be one of his fighting slaves, I suspect. That boy really took a shine to that ol' girl," he chuckled mockingly.

Ramses reached down to Captain Fletcher's waist and unbuckled his holster belt, which held his custom shotgun pistols. He slung them around his own waist and buckled them.

Suddenly, four crewmen ran onto the deck with muskets held at the ready.

Ramses saw them and swiftly pulled one of Captain Fletcher's shotgun pistols from its holster with his right hand and cut all four of the crewmen down with one shot from its barrel.

Each man was struck by multiple projectiles, which forcefully knocked them backwards, into the deck, in an array of motionless postures.

Ramses looked down at the smoking custom pistol and grinned before removing the second custom pistol from the left side of the holster and raised it to Captain Fletcher's trembling head.

Captain Fletcher nervously raised his hands again in surrender.

"But... you said that you would not kill me!" Ramses turned to Scars and smiled sinisterly. Scars grabbed the captain and dragged him over to the cargo hold. He looked him in the face.

"I will see you in hell, Captain Fletcher!" Scars held the captain by his collar as he hung over the opening of the hold.

Captain Fletcher peered down into the bowels of his ship and saw the hundreds of Africans that he'd held in captivity. Each one with seething hatred in their eyes as they desperately reached up for him.

Ramses stood next to Scars as he let go of the captain's collar and allowed him to fall into the awaiting hands of the Africans still chained in the hold. He was held in the air by the many hands of his captors and passed around.

Captain Fletcher reached desperately for the opening as he screamed in terror before he disappeared under the mass of bodies of the captive Africans.

Scars and Ramses were making their way to the longboat when they heard Captain Fletcher's screams of agony as the Africans literally ripped him apart, limb from limb.

CHAPTER 18

NAIRA

Aboard the *Bayou Belle*, Fulani sat alone in a cabin below deck. She still wore her Mortisi battle kit. Her right ankle was chained to the bottom of a small cot, which was securely fastened to the hull of the ship by thick, half-inch bolts on all four legs. She concentrated on the sounds of the different crewmen's voices above deck, attempting to get an accurate count of the number of men she would have to kill to escape. But they had been at sea for months. Even if she were successful in killing them all, *where would she go*? And more importantly, *how would she get there*, she thought. Fulani decided to bide her time until they reached land and somehow escape-- even if it meant her life.

The crewmen had been drinking and singing for most of the day. The room she was being held in was full of fine gold and silver trinkets, the quality of which she had never seen the likes.

Atop an ornate dresser against the opposite wall of the cot were an assorted array of gold necklaces and baubles of all shapes and sizes.

Fulani was not interested in any of the treasure that was at her disposal. All she thought of for the duration of her captivity was her father, her brother's betrayal and the last time she held Bambara in her arms.

Her thoughts were interrupted by a sudden knock on her cabin door. Then an all too familiar voice rang out, "Princess, may I come in?" he asked in a subtle voice, as if she could understand his words.

Fulani could tell by the tenor of his voice that he too had been drinking and was now completely inebriated. In the times before this when he drank, the captain would always come down below and attempt to woo her, a proposition that she vowed never to accept. He would have to rape her, if she was not able to kill him first.

"Fulani... Fulani... I know you can hear me!" Captain Bishop yelled through the door before entering the cabin.

"I have brought a gift for you, so that you and

I will be able to communicate, my dark chocolate vixen!"

Fulani glared at the captain as he entered the room. She could not understand a word he was saying and actually did not care to.

Captain Bishop stood in the doorway, seemingly pleased with himself.

"I have brought you a gift," he repeated drunkenly, before turning back to the door and putting his right hand out towards it.

After a few brief moments, in walked a frail African girl just blossoming into early womanhood. She sheepishly entered Fulani's cabin and took the captain's hand timidly. The girl bowed toward Fulani respectfully, then spoke in Ashanti to her.

"Greetings, my Princess. I am happy to see that you still thrive. Our predicament is a terrible one, but we must survive by our wits. I will do anything I can to assist you. This colorless animal has no idea what I am saying, so you and I can communicate without fear of punishment. I long for the day we can return to our beloved Ashantiland, but until then, we must survive."

Fulani perked up as she stared at the young

girl suspiciously. It had been over three months since she'd heard her own language spoken. Her native tongue calmed her spirit for one fleeting moment before she became guarded once more. The young girl continued.

"I understand why you are apprehensive about trusting me, but I assure you that I still have the heart and soul of an Ashanti!"

Fulani climbed off the cot and stood as she stared at the girl. "What are you called?" she asked suspiciously in Ashanti.

Captain Bishop looked down at the African girl eagerly.

"What did she say? Well, what did she say?"

The girl looked up at him and answered in English with a thick African accent.

"She asked me my name, Master Bishop."

He lifted his head and looked over at Fulani excited. "Well tell her, girl! Tell her your name," he commanded eagerly.

"I am called Lisa by the godless ones," she answered Fulani soft and timid.

Fulani scoffed and frowned at the girl.

"No! I want to know what your mother and father called you?"

Lisa looked up at Captain Bishop frightened to respond. She took a deep breath and answered.

"My given name is Naira, my Princess."

Fulani nodded respectfully toward Naira.

"Naira, that is a beautiful name."

Fulani sat back on the cot.

Captain Bishop was becoming impatient.

"Tell her what I say, girl!"

Naira nodded her head rapidly to him.

"I would like for you and I to put the past behind us. I know that it will take time for you to trust me, but I think in time... you will see that I am not the monster you think I am."

He turned and looked at Naira and impatiently waited for her to translate his words to Fulani. Once Fulani heard his words translated, she broke out into mocking laughter.

Naira backed away from the captain, who turned red in anger and embarrassment. He stepped towards Fulani aggressively and raised his right hand to strike her.

Fulani leaped from the cot and took a defensive but aggressive posture towards him. She looked quickly over to the quivering translator.

"Speak my words to this filthy barbarian!" Naira nodded to Fulani rapidly.

"If you ever lay your filthy hands upon me, I will slit your throat from ear to ear!" she barked then spat on the floor in front of Captain Bishop's feet.

Naira nervously translated Fulani's words to him. Captain Bishop raised his right hand higher, then thought for a brief moment before slowly lowering his right hand. He looked at Fulani lustfully.

"My oh my, ain't you something! I knew it when I first laid eyes on you. I said to myself, '*Now there is a warrior.*' It's that very sentiment that is going to make me a rich man. No, I'm not going to put my hands on you yet, but if you don't win for me..." He walked straight up to her face. "... I will put your black ass on the auction block as a two-cock-at-a-time bed wench!"

Naira stopped translating at the vulgar part of the captain's threat.

Fulani knowing he said more, ordered Naira to translate every word he said to her. Naira complied and finished the translation.

Fulani's face remained stoic as she listened and glared at Captain Bishop. The captain backed out of the cabin, but before passing through the threshold, he spoke again.

"We shall see what you are made of in the morning. There will be a competition of sorts. So, sleep well, Princess... Sleep well."

Naira translated the last of the captain's words to Fulani with a worried look on her face. She bowed to Fulani, then started to walk out. Fulani grabbed her by the arm and looked into her face determined.

"I promise you, I will find a way for us to escape this place. Do not lose heart, Little One."

Naira looked up at Fulani.

"Thank you, my Princess, for your concern, but, I think it would be more prudent for you to think of what awaits you in the morning. You are not the only skilled fighter on this vessel and tomorrow each and every one of you will fight to see who is worthy to remain on this ship. May Nyame the Great protect you, my Princess."

A tear trailed down her cheek as she ran out of the cabin and closed the door behind her on the way out.

CHAPTER 19

FIGHT OR SWIM

Morning came quicker than usual, it seemed to Fulani. Wearing her Mortisi battle kit, she knelt by the cot with her hands raised out to her sides as she prayed to Nyame for strength and protection.

"Oh, Great One, you who knows and sees all. Please grant me the strength to vanquish my enemies. Know that what I am about to do, I do with the heaviest of hearts. I have..."

Fulani stopped in mid-sentence and buckled over with discomfort in her stomach. The pain felt like an intense cramp that would not subside. She became disoriented and felt as if she was going to be sick, pass out, or both. Fulani breathed deeply, and took as much air into her lungs as she could manage periodically, then exhaled slowly. She repeated this breathing pattern for a minute or so, while pondering what could possibly make her feel that terrible and that sick, so fast.

"Maybe I've caught some type of illness from the barbarians," she thought.

Continuing to breathe deeply and exhale slowly, Fulani's ailment had seemed to dissipate for a few fleeting moments before she jumped up and vomited uncontrollably in a corner of the cabin. She was throwing up still when Naira knocked gently on the door. Unable to stop throwing up, Fulani ignored the knocks.

Naira entered the room cautiously and was startled by what she saw. Quickly, she ran over to Fulani to assist her. Fulani threw up once more before standing up and trying to clear her head. Naira took her by the arm and helped her to the cot to take a seat. She fanned Fulani with the bottom of her dress and tried to give her some extra air.

Fulani looked up at her confused.

"Thank you, Naira. I don't know what came over me. I feel better now."

Naira placed her right hand gently onto Fulani's sweaty forehead to check if she had a fever of some kind. But her skin was cool to the touch. She looked at Fulani's face.

"My Princess, how long has it been since the red river flowed from your body?"

Fulani frowned, confused and a little embarrassed at Naira's question.

"Red river, what are you talking about, Little One?"

"My Princess, I mean not to offend, but the red river that flows from women every month."

Fulani thought for a moment, then, finally understood what Naira was trying to ask her.

"But, that was impossible!" she thought, *"I have only been with one man and that was..."*

Fulani counted the months rapidly in her head and realized that she and Bambara had been together by the river almost three months prior to this very day. Distraught, she returned to the cot and fell face first onto it in despair.

Naira slowly walked over to Fulani and rubbed her back softly in an attempt to console her.

Fulani rolled over. "How can I bring a child into this madness? My future is uncertain. A child would only make matters worse!"

She stared at the ceiling.

"Nyame! Why have you abandoned me?"

Naira thought, then stood aggressively.

"Forgive me, my Princess. But you having a life inside you may be the least of your worries. You will be fighting for your life in only a few short moments! You must concentrate on your own survival, before you can worry about a life that has not entered the world yet! You and I are in a sea of uncertainty and despair. We must navigate these waters together with cunning and strength. In my village, we female children would often hear tales of your mother, Sumitra the Mighty, and her prowess as a warrior. If there be any of her in you, we should be able to vanquish anyone they put in front of you today! This is all you should be concentrating on, my Princess." Naira proclaimed.

Fulani wiped the tears from her eyes and stood. She did not say anything, but in her head were images of her mother, Sumitra, training her with her Tutsi sickle knives on the beach when she was a little girl. Fulani felt her mother's spirit and her despair became intense anger and confidence. She dropped to her knees and spread her arms out to her sides.

Naira smiled and dropped to her knees beside

Fulani.

"Nyame, I am Princes Fulani of the Ashanti, daughter of Chief Yoruba and Queen Sumitra. Hear me now! I will not despair any longer. I will accept this path that you have laid before me. But I will leave a swath of death the likes of which have not been seen on this side of the great river. To this I swear on the blood of my ancestors and the life of my unborn child!"

Suddenly, the door swung open. Two large crewmen entered the cabin.

"Time to find out what your're made of, Princess," said the short filthy crewman to the left of the doorway. The second crewman was as unkempt as the one in the door. He entered the cabin cautiously, knelt down and unlocked the shackle on Fulani's ankle. The crewman kept a watchful eye on her as he backed away nervously.

Fulani smirked, stood and turned to face them. She took a deep breath and nodded to Naira, who was trembling, and winked before trotting out of the cabin like a pugilist on her way to the ring.

Fulani trotted fearlessly down the dark hall to

the main hold. The early morning sunrays beamed through every available crevice and she could hear the murmurings of many crewmen who had gathered to watch the spectacle.

Fulani tried to heed Naira's advice and only concentrate on the battle at hand, but all she could think about was the young one inside of her. She tried to shake herself into the proper mindset before she reached the area where the fights were to take place.

The hallway opened into the main hold. Fulani's eyes were very sensitive to the light because she had been locked below decks for so long. She blinked rapidly until her pupils adjusted. Once she could see properly, Fulani looked up at the crowd of crewmen on the edges of the hold above where she was standing.

Many of the crewmen catcalled and jeered at her from their perches as they passed around a jug of whiskey from one man to the other.

On the walls inside the hold were the other captive Africans including men, women and small children. Terrified, they all remained silent with their heads lowered, too afraid to lift them.

Naira walked up behind Fulani so she could

translate to her. A few moments later the other combatants were lead to the main hold where Fulani waited. She turned and watched as the largest African woman she had ever seen entered the hold. The woman had bushy hair and eyebrows and wore a wild, insane look in her eyes. She glared at Fulani as she passed. Her arms were larger than Fulani's thighs. Nonetheless, Fulani returned the glare, unintimidated. The sensation was just what she needed to focus on the situation at hand. She closed her eyes and breathed deeply. When she opened them again, it was just in time to see the second warrior enter the hold.

The warrior was a handsome, young, African man who had been obviously beaten into submission. His left eye was badly swollen. His forehead was covered in dried blood and he walked with a severe limp.

The young warrior reminded Fulani of her beloved Bambara. She tried desperately to suppress her emotions because she knew there was a strong possibility that she and the young warrior would have to try to kill one another in a matter of minutes.

The third combatant entered the hold with no guards. She was a beautiful Latina who was a light shade of brown with long thick black flowing hair. Her cocoa colored face had a couple of thin scars from previous battles on it, as did her body. She was chiseled, as if she had been sculpted. The beautiful warrior brushed past Fulani, as she exaggeratedly confidently swished her ass from side to side with each step. She knew how to play up to the crewmen and did so with great commotion. The crewmen cheered and whistled as she whipped them up into a carnal frenzy.

The warrior took her place on the line next to the wounded warrior, looked him up and down and scoffed. She then turned her attention to Fulani who was still looking at her. The Latina warrior glared back at Fulani before reaching down and lifting her tiny leather loincloth, exposing her clean-shaven vagina.

The crew went absalutely wild as she raised her arms in the air and played up to them once more. Slowly, she turned back and gazed at Fulani, then licked her lips seductively at her.

Fulani ignored the woman's overtures and

tried to remain focused. She turned slightly toward Naira.

"Who is that vulgar woman?"

"Carlota is her name, but in the pit she is known simply as 'The Brazilian'. She has been fighting for Captain Bishop for two years. Do not underestimate her, Princess. She is as deadly as she is promiscuous."

Carlota took her place next to the other two warriors, but continued to glare at Fulani. The princess stared back at her, unimpressed.

A few moments passed before the sound of heavy chains scraping against the deck of the ship could be heard down the hall. Three crewmen appeared in the main hold dragging a large wriggling burlap sack that was wrapped almost totally in chains. The three men struggled to drag the sack.

Fulani noticed that the sack was moving. Her curiosity peaked as she watched them drag it to the center of the hold.

One of the three crewmen nervously removed the key ring from his belt. He fumbled with the other keys as he attempted to locate the correct one to open the lock. Shaking, the man placed the key into the lock and turned it timidly. The other two crewmen backed away nervously as he did so.

Suddenly, the lock clicked open and the chains fell from the sack. When the contents of the sack fell out, everyone who had gathered could not believe their eyes. The crew, the large female warrior and the Brazilian laughed hysterically at the sight.

A dark-skinned African who stood only four feet tall tumbled to the deck. He wore a zebra hide loincloth. His demeanor was fierce. He growled like a wild animal and flailed his arms angrily at the crowd, as he craned his neck from one side to the other, threateningly.

Naira looked at the man in shock. "What is he?" she asked Fulani without taking her eyes off the tiny man. Fulani marveled at the small man's muscular physique as well before answering. "I remember stories my mother told me as a child about a tribe of tiny Africans who dwelled in the deepest part of the jungle. She also stressed the fact that they were as fearsome, as they were small and were not to be trifled with. But today is the first time I have ever seen one. She called them... Pygmies."

The crewman with the key approached the Pygmy. The Pygmy jumped and turned quickly. He looked at the crewman ominously. In the blink of an eye, the little man ran toward him and scurried up his body, as if climbing the trunk of a tree. The crewman swung his arms and spun around as he struggled to remove the tiny warrior from his chest.

Finally, the Pygmy grabbed hold of the back of the crewman's neck and plunged his face into the left side of his head. The little warrior opened his mouth as wide as it would stretch and revealed two rows of jagged teeth that had been filed down to razor sharp points. He sunk his teeth deep into the crewman's ear and ripped it from the side of his head with ease.

Blood gushed from the resulting hole in crewman's head. He screamed in agony as the Pygmy swiftly released his grip on the wounded man's neck.

The crewman's bloody ear dangled from his mouth as he dropped back to the deck, landing on his feet. The Pygmy turned and looked at the crowd in a crazed state and spit the ear at the jeering crew, then flailed his arms angrily at them. He berated every one of the faces of his captors in an African dialect that even Naira could not understand. The Pygmy pounded his chest.

"Demons! Demons! I am Nkosi the Great! I swear on the lives of the ones who came before and the ones who bore me! I shall kill each one of you slowly and roast your worthless hides in my war fires!"

He quickly spun around and glared at Captain Bishop. The Pygmy lifted his well-defined right arm and pointed at the captain with all of the conviction he possessed.

"But you! You will die at my hand then I will dine on your corpse, never allowing your spirit to find peace in the afterlife!"

The earless crewman writhed in pain as the other two crewmen ran over to assist him. He looked back at the Pygmy with fear in his eyes as they led him out of the hold.

The crew booed, cursed and threw whatever they could find at the Pygmy.

Suddenly, Captain Bishop moved toward Nkosi aggressively, as he wielded a thick leather bullwhip in his right hand. He lifted his hand and twirled it above his head effortlessly then cracked it across the right shoulder of Nkosi, leaving a bloody open gash upon him. The captain glared threateningly at Nkosi as he swung the whip over his head again. The small warrior cowered in pain and placed his hand over the laceration left by the bullwhip. Nkosi attempted to block out the pain and took a step in the direction of Captain Bishop. He glanced to his right and looked at Fulani.

Fulani knew that Nkosi was about to attack Captain Bishop, an act that would surely cost him his life. She did not want to see such a fate befall such a brave and honorable warrior. Fulani, as undetectably as she could, shook her head no at the poised little warrior.

Nkosi was beside himself with rage. He defiantly growled at the captain like a wild beast and continued to glare at him menacingly before he complied and took his place in line beside the Brazilian.

Captain Bishop cracked the whip toward the warriors who stood before him in the line. He walked toward each one of them and stared directly into their faces. Slowly he turned and glared at Fulani, who was still trying to grasp everything that was happening around her. The captain raised his right hand, then his pointer finger. He gestured his finger, signaling for Fulani and Naira to come to him. Nervously, Naira turned to Fulani.

"You must take your place on the line, my Princess."

Fulani nodded to her, then walked fearlessly to the spot next to the Pygmy and stood, glaring at Captain Bishop. The captain walked over to Fulani and smiled. Fulani rolled her eyes in disgust. Captain Bishop backed away from her and lifted his hands into the air before addressing his crew. Naira quickly made her way over to Fulani's left so she could translate for her.

"Welcome to another rendition of 'Fight or Swim'," the captain announced as if he were the ringmaster at a circus.

The crewmen that surrounded the edge of the hold went into a frenzy of clapping, whistling, and cheering, as the captain continued.

"Here is where we find out who will be coming to shore as a representative of the great

Bishop Plantation... and who will merely stay on shore and become fish food!"

Naira translated to Fulani and the others as fast as she could. The Brazilian stood confidently with a smirk on her face. She raised her right hand and waved to the crowd of crewmen before leaning forward to throw an intimidating look at Fulani. Sensing the Brazilian glaring at her, Fulani leaned forward and threw an unafraid gaze back at the Brazilian.

As Captain Bishop turned back to the captive warriors, he noticed the brewing animosity between the Brazilian and Fulani.

"Ahhhh look... we already have two combatants ready to have at one another! You two will have to wait your turn," he chided playfully, while simultaneously waving his finger at them.

The Brazilian, her frustration obvious, sighed, as she stood straight again. Fulani stood straight again as well while the captain continued.

"The first combatants will be Fatima and the Zulu!"

The large woman heard her name and anxiously jumped out of the line. She lumbered to the side of Captain Bishop and scanned the remaining warriors in the line. The male warrior, who had been beaten, limped off the line and made his way toward the center of the hold to face her. Captain Bishop backed away slowly and raised his left hand into the air.

"When I drop my hand, the contest will begin!"

The captain turned his head in the direction of Naira awaiting her translation. Once she was finished, she turned to the captain and nodded.

Fatima breathed heavily as she got ready to attack the wounded warrior. The warrior turned to Fatima and just stood there. He did not get into any type of prepared stance. Fatima grinned sinisterly as she awaited the signal from Captain Bishop to begin.

The wounded warrior glanced at Fulani and trained his sad eyes on her. The look on his face was one of intense sorrow and eminent relief. Fulani felt a kinship with the warrior in that brief moment. She could see in his eyes that he had lost his will to live. A sentiment she knew all too well. She stood there trying to convey how sorry she was for him through her eyes.

The warrior, feeling her compassion, nodded to her respectfully as the captain cracked the whip to signal the contest to begin.

The crewmen cheered rambunctiously as Fatima lumbered toward the wounded warrior who still had his eyes trained on Fulani. The warrior did not try to defend himself. His body went numb as he closed his eyes.

Fatima grabbed him, spun him around and snapped his neck like a twig with her huge hands. He dropped to the deck with a thud, lifeless.

Naira cringed in horror, while Fatima reveled in her unopposed victory. She pranced around the center of hold with her arms raised.

Fulani was infuriated. She jumped out of line and into the center of the hold behind Fatima. Fatima turned and saw Fulani staring at her with rage in her eyes. She pointed to the corpse of the warrior she had just dispatched, then pointed at Fulani, motioning to her that she was about to receive the same treatment as he.

Fulani smirked at the enormous woman as she got into her fighting stance with calm. Once prepared, Fulani lifted her pointer finger and signaled the snarling Fatima to come to her.

Fatima hesitated, then looked over at Captain Bishop confused.

Captain Bishop laughed excitedly before addressing the crew once more.

"Well, boys! It looks like we have ourselves a challenge! In all my years, I have not seen someone so ready to die! So be it, Princess, if that's what you wish! This pains me deeply, because I had such plans for you!"

Naira translated feverishly his every word to Fulani. Fulani turned her head slightly toward Naira. "Translate this to that colorless dog!" Naira chuckled into her hand then looked around timidly, hoping the captain would not ask her what she found so humorous. She quickly recomposed herself and nodded her head rapidly before answering Fulani's command.

"Yes, my Princess!"

"If you are so sure I am throwing my life away, then why don't you wager on this mindless hippo?"

Captain Bishop stopped playing up to the crew and thought seriously about Fulani's proposal.

"What type of wager did you have in mind, Princess?"

Fulani kept her eyes locked on Fatima, who was drooling from the mouth as she glared back at her.

"When I send this beast back to the underworld, Lisa will be allowed to be my companion for the duration of our time with you, here on this wretched ship and when we reach your accursed lands!"

The captain smirked before he answered, "Done!"

Fulani continued. "Secondly, I will receive proper care until the life I carry inside me is born!"

Naira translated quickly.

Captain Bishop was flabbergasted. His face turned a light shade of red as he removed his hat and twirled it around in his hands with a startled look on his face.

"A life inside you, huh?"

His response was one of shock, with a hint of jealousy.

"That huge buck? That Bambara? Is he the father of the child you carry?"

Fulani turned to him.

"By the grace of Nyame the Almighty, yes he is!"

Captain Bishop scratched his head as he tried desperately to conceal his disappointment. He seemed more like a jilted lover than a slave master.

"Well now, you are full of surprises."

He looked at Naira.

"Is that all miss high and mighty would like, or is there something else before we get started? How about daily foot massages or perhaps breakfast in bed?" he chuckled at his own attempt at humor, but he was secretly seething inside.

Naira translated Captain Bishop's response to Fulani, then paused as she awaited her answer. Fulani thought hard, then spoke again.

"I would also like his word, that once my child is born, I will be allowed to raise it myself!"

When Naira finished translating Fulani's last request, the captain scoffed.

"If I thought you were going to survive Fatima, I would never make such promises. But my mother always said I have a sporting nature. I give you my word as a gentleman, for all the good it will do you after Fatima rips your black ass apart!"

Captain Bishop mockingly bowed to Fulani before he again raised his arms and started getting his crew riled up for the upcoming fight. He turned back to Fulani and reiterated his statement.

"Yes, Princess, you have my word!"

Naira translated the captain's last statement.

Fulani nodded to him. When she did, a strange calm came over her. She closed her eyes and concentrated on her breathing. The princess opened them again and imagined where and how she would attack this sizable warrior who outweighed her by at least the weight of another woman.

Captain Fletcher raised his right hand with the whip and prepared to give the signal to begin. He again mocked Fulani by making the sign of the cross across his chest before he cracked the bullwhip.

"Begin!"

Fatima charged Fulani, growling and grunting

as she approached. Although Fulani could feel the deck vibrate beneath her feet each time Fatima took a step towards her, she remained calm and waited on Fatima to reach her.

Fatima raised her huge arms and clenched her fists as she prepared to hammer Fulani into the deck like a nail.

Naira horrified, shut her eyes as tightly as she could. She could not bring herself to watch Fulani die.

Every crewman cheered as they stood in anticipation of bloodshed.

Captain Bishop stood to the side nervously as Fatima attacked. He wanted to put a stop to the match, but dared not, because his men would know how he really felt about Fulani.

Fulani stood in the center of the hold fearlessly and waited for Fatima to lumber into range. Once Fatima was close enough, Fulani jabbed her sharply with a left to the nose and danced away quickly.

Fatima stunned, raised her right hand to her nose and discovered it was bleeding. She became more furious as she spun around to face the dancing-on-her-toes-smugly Fulani.

Fulani held her right hand back and up near her face, while her left hand she held slightly further out and awaited the behemoth's next advance.

Fatima screamed angrily at the top of her lungs before charging the awaiting Fulani once more. Fulani side stepped Fatima and hit her with a lightning fast two punch combination to the side of the huge warrior's head.

Fatima lumbered clumsily past Fulani. She turned again quickly and tried to grab the elusive princess. It was the moment Fulani was waiting for. She saw that all of the giant warrior's weight was now on her lead leg, so she swiftly lifted her right leg high into the air and brought her heel down on Fatima's left knee as hard as she could.

The force of the blow, combined with the momentum of such a large woman, proved to be devastating.

Fatima's knee was dislocated instantly. Everyone watching heard the knee pop and gasped as she tumbled to the deck in excruciating pain. She screamed in agony and grabbed her damaged knee with both hands as her momentum sent her into an involuntary roll on the floor.

Fulani slid to the side as the behemoth rolled passed her. She kept her eyes trained on Captain Bishop as she calmly walked over to Fatima and mounted her from behind. Fatima whimpered and begged for mercy in her native language. Fulani ignored her pleas, as she filled both hands with Fatima's hair. Emotionless, Fulani rammed Fatima's face forcefully down into the deck as she glared at the captain. She forced her face into the deck over and over and over again, turning Fatima's face into a bloody mess. Each time she forced Fatima's face into the deck, memories of her love, her home and her life flashed through her mind's eye. Fulani became more enraged. She finally stopped when Fatima's body no longer moved. Fulani regained her composure as she stood straddling Fatima's lifeless body. She continued to glare at the captain as she breathed heavily.

The crewmen who witnessed the unbelievable display of fighting skill were stunned and dead silent. After a few moments of processing what they had just seen, one by one, each man stood and began to clap and cheer. Finally, more rum was poured and lifted to her incredible victory.

Captain Bishop clapped slowly as he walked toward Fulani. Once he reached her, he said nothing. He just lifted her right arm into the air. The crewmen cheered louder for her than before.

Naira opened her eyes and was delighted to see that Fulani was not killed. She clapped excitedly. Carlota was furious. She acrobatically flipped off the line toward where Fulani stood triumphantly over Fatima. Swiftly, Fulani spun toward the backflipping Carlota prepared in her battle stance.

Suddenly, Captain Bishop cracked his bullwhip across the body of Carlota in mid-flip and she tumbled uncontrollably to the deck. She jumped to her feet and glared at the captain defiantly, as she breathed heavily.

Fulani turned and looked at Captain Bishop surprised. The captain walked calmly toward Carlota as he slowly wrapped the whip around his right hand.

"The next one of you to act without my order to do so will be given to my crew as a plaything until we reach Carolina, then thrown to the fucking sharks! Is that clear?" he growled.

Carlota lowered her head and backed up quickly to her place next to the Pygmy in line. Once there, she lifted her head and gave a cold stare to Fulani.

Captain Bishop kept his eyes trained on Carlota. "That's better," he said as he made his way over to her.

Fulani stepped over Fatima's body and calmly walked to the line, turned and stood beside the seething Brazilian.

Naira quickly made her way beside Fulani to translate. She could hardly contain the relief she felt inside because of the princess' victory in battle. She was very pleased that she now had a companion for the terrible ordeal they found themselves in.

Captain Bishop stood in front of Carlota and Fulani and admired them for a moment before addressing them again. He only spoke loud enough for them to hear.

"I want you two to find a way to coexist for now. Truth be told, I would love to see which of you wild bitches is the best. But what good is that if there is no one here to pay me to see it?" he asked excitedly. Naira translated to Fulani, who hung on every word from her mouth.

"So, for now you are allies, until I tell you you're not. Do you understand?" asked the captain in an authoritative tone.

Carlota scoffed defiantly. He let his whip hit the floor once more. Carlota reluctantly nodded that she understood. Fulani smirked evilly, then nodded as well.

Captain Bishop's scowl quickly became a wide smile as he spun around and walked away. He turned to his first mate standing near him.

"I want both of them prepared and brought to my quarters tonight."

The first mate nodded to him and pointed to the crewmen who had brought the Pygmy to the hold. With only a hand gesture they understood and quickly grabbed Fulani and the Brazilian to take them back to their cabins.

Naira followed closely behind with concern on her face.

CHAPTER 20

GOING TO DIE ON THIS NIGHT

Ramses and Scars struggled to row the longboat on the stormy sea. Behind them in the distance, the *Carolina Gold* was forced into the reef by the gale force winds and strong current. The hull splintered easily on the sharp coral as the main mast crashed into the sea. The remainder of the vessel began to sink into the dark, murky storm churned ocean.

Ramses rowed as fast and as hard as he could.

"Looks like you and me going to die on this night! So, I have a question?"

"I believe you may be correct! So, ask away!" Scars shouted in response, as he rowed frantically.

"Why did you help me escape? Secondly, why did you teach me your words?"

Scars thought briefly before he answered.

"I did it because... I did it because... this is going to sound silly, but, I admire you!"

Ramses looked puzzled.

"Admire me? Why?"

Scars stopped rowing.

"You and your men were willing to die for your freedom! But I, on the other hand, accepted it without so much as a harsh word in protest! You made me ashamed of myself!"

Scars began to row hard once more.

Ramses thought about what Scars had told him before he started to row fiercely once more and for the first time, since he had been taken for the second time, a prideful smile spread across his face.

"Scars, my friend, it is not where you start from. It is how you finish which determines your worth!"

Scars nodded to Ramses and the two of them continued to row through the large swells and high winds, together. As the two of them rowed an ominously huge rogue wave appeared on the dark horizon.

Scars turned his head to the left and watched in horror as the wave rose from the depths like a leviathan destined to engulf his and Ramses' tiny longboat.

Ramses caught the dark shape of the wave in his peripheral and turned. He marveled at the awesome display of Nyame's power.

"Row, Ramses! Row!" yelled Scars desperately.

Ramses and Scars rowed as hard and as fast as they could, but it was to no avail. They realized they could not outrow the rogue wave.

Ramses abruptly stopped rowing and stood in the boat to face the wave and his death on his feet like a true Mandinkan warrior. He lifted his hands to the heavens and closed his eyes.

"I will always love you, Fulani," he shouted into the night sky.

Scars was not so prepared to meet his maker. He rowed frantically by himself until their small boat was engulfed by the thirty foot wall of water.

~

The following day the sea was very calm and the sun shined brightly on a pristine beach of white sand. Seagulls spread their wings and glided on the warm updrafts as they swooped down low over the shallows, hunting for a feeder-fish meal. Other native fowl chirped and sang perched in huge palm trees, which dotted the small island as far as the eye could see. A flock of pink flamingos were startled and took off in unison in an awesome spectacle of pink and white through the sky. Small waves gently rolled onto shore.

Debris from the Carolina Gold, such as broken sections of rope, splintered pieces of wood from the ship's hull, and the bloated bodies of dead crewmen and African captors, were strewn along the shoreline.

The longboat Ramses and Scars escaped in lay on the beach upside down and partially buried in sand. Ramses and Scars lay on opposite sides of the boat, unconscious.

Ramses' eyes opened slowly. He blinked a few times as he attempted to focus. Pushing himself to his feet, he grabbed his aching head and looked around the small island. Ramses turned and looked out to sea. It was low tide and the hulking wreckage of the *Carolina Gold* was broken upon the reef a few miles off the same shore he was looking from.

Ramses dropped to his knees and lifted his

hands over his head then closed his eyes tightly before beginning to pray humbly.

"I am not worthy of your protection. I thank you, Nyame! Please protect Fulani, wherever she may be. Please give me all the strength and means to find her!"

He stood, turned and walked back toward the buried longboat. Ramses bent at the knees and rolled Scars over. Gently, he slapped Scars in the face, trying to revive him. Scars did not respond and remained unconscious.

Worried, Ramses ran over to the water's edge and scooped some into his cupped hands. He turned and quickly, but very carefully carried the water to Scars and threw the water into the face of his friend.

Scars awoke immediately, shaking his head. He opened his eyes and saw a smiling Ramses staring at him.

"If this is heaven, I'm fucking disappointed," he joked weakly.

Ramses stood and extended his right hand to Scars to help him up off the ground. Scars grabbed Ramses' outstretched hand and was helped to his feet. He brushed the sand off his body and assessed their new surroundings.

Ramses looked at Scars quizzically and concerned.

"Do you have any idea where we could possibly be?"

Scars looked into the sky. He bent down and grabbed a fistful of sand, then slowly poured it out of his hand.

"If I had to guess, I would say somewhere off the coast of Florida, maybe."

Ramses glared at Scars concerned.

"Florida? Where is dis Florida? How far is dis place from mother Africa?"

Scars stood up straight and walked over to Ramses to console him.

"I'm sorry my friend... but, we are far away from your homeland. We are in the Americas, the land of the not so free and the home of the slave," Scars chuckled.

Ramses turned to him scowling.

"Do you mean this is the land where they bring my people to enslave them?" he inquired angrily.

Seeing Ramses' agitation, Scars was careful not to make light of the situation again.

"That is correct, my friend. This is where many of the people from your homeland are brought to be free labor for the money grubbing plantation owners. Fortunately, all of that is over for us now. You and I have escaped all of that unpleasantness. By the look of things, we are kind of sitting pretty here!"

Ramses did not understand Scars' inference, so he frowned his face in confusion. Scars saw that Ramses did not understand what *sitting pretty* meant.

"What I mean to say is that I am sure there is fresh water around here somewhere; we have plenty of fish to catch and, last but not least, we are free to do whatever the hell we want! The only thing missing, and these are very important so pay attention... are big, beautiful bodied women!" Scars clapped his hands excitedly and chuckled.

Ramses turned and looked out into the vast ocean and thought hard for a second. He turned back to Scars wearing a determined look.

"There will be no freedom for me until I find Fulani," he declared in deadly seriousness.

Scars walked closer to Ramses. "Look, big

fella, you don't even know where they have taken her. She could be anywhere! You do understand the term anywhere, right? Hell, for all you know, she could be dead!"

Without warning Ramses turned and jumped on top of Scars. He glanced quickly to his right and saw a large seashell within his reach. Ramses held the struggling Scars with his left arm and grabbed the shell with his right hand. He put the sharpest end of the shell to the protesting Scar's throat, before slowly getting face-to-face and staring into Scars' eyes, intimidatingly.

"Fulani is not dead! I do not want you to say that to me ever again! Do you understand? I will find her and she and I will return home, together!" Ramses rebutted furiously.

Scars pushed Ramses' hand away from his throat cautiously and slowly.

"Okay, okay, big fella! I believe you, calm down! May I?" Scars motioned to Ramses to allow him to get up.

Ramses calmed himself, then stood up, allowing Scars to get out of the sand. Relieved, Scars got up off the ground but was careful not to enrage Ramses again. He brushed the sand from his clothing before taking a different approach in their conversation.

"Although, from what I could tell, your significant other was a very special woman indeed! If I were a betting man, which indeed I am, I'd bet that your beloved Fulani has been taken to Bishop's fighters' farm down in the Carolinas."

Ramses grew excited.

"Then that is where we will go!"

Scars scratched his head quizzically, then walked back over to Ramses more serious than before.

"Ramses, it is not going to be that easy. You are talking about trying to find a black needle in a lily-white, hateful haystack in the Deep South, no less!"

Ramses glared at Scars with all the determination he possessed.

"That is exactly what we are going to do!"

Scars thought to himself while looking down at the white sand. He pondered for a moment and kicked the sand around with his foot a bit. Finally, he took a deep breath and held it, then exhaled and sighed.

"Fuck it all, I'm in!"

Scars smiled and mockingly saluted Ramses. He stood playfully at attention.

"What is your first order? uhhhhh, Captain Ramses, sir!"

Ramses smirked at Scars before turning in place and surveying the island at a glance.

"The first thing we should do is find a consistent fresh water source. Secondly, find food. Then, we build a strong shelter. Then, you and I must learn everything about this place. Then, we will find Fulani. Ramses will teach you to fight properly, as the Mortisi do... and you will teach Ramses everything you know about this America and its people."

Scars grinned widely, clapped his hands once and rubbed them together eagerly.

"Captain Ramses, by the time I get through with you, the only way people will know that you are not a proper gentleman will be by the color of your skin and nothing more. When would you like to initiate this new plan, Cap?"

Ramses turned around and faced the sea. In his mind were only thoughts of Fulani. He lowered his head and sighed deeply before lifting it again wearing the fierce look of determination.

"We will start immediately!"

CHAPTER 21

MAROONED

Ramses and Scars began to improve their situation on the island by taking care of the three most important elements of survival: water, food and shelter. The two of them chopped at the base of a large palm tree with two boarding axes they'd found in some of the debris from the *Carolina Gold*, which washed up on the beach on a daily basis.

The two of them began to form a kinship that neither one of them had known before. At the tree, Ramses chopped first, then Scars. Each of them chopped at the tree three times until it began to topple.

Scars, who was not accustomed to manual labor of any kind, watched proudly as the palm tree fell. He grinned widely. Once down the two men limbed it, then carried a large section of the tree to one of the many holes they had dug in the sand. Both of them were soaked with sweat as they toiled in the unforgiving sun of the Florida Keys. Carefully, they strained their muscles to drop the tree into one of the holes and turned back around to retrieve another.

Ramses and Scars stood in a shallow canal. Each man held a handmade fishing spear that Ramses had fashioned from wild bamboo, which was plentiful on their little paradise. Both men stood motionless with their arms cocked back prepared to throw as they stalked the shallow water for fish.

Ramses skillfully thrust his fishing spear into the water with lightning quick speed. He pulled the spear out and revealed a large colorful fish wriggling on the end of it. Lifting his catch out of the water, he smiled widely and mocked Scars as he effortlessly tossed the fish off his spear onto the sandy bank.

Scars scowled at Ramses. He sighed frustrated and again trained his eyes back down at the water. He was startled at the sight of a large fish and prepared to strike with his spear. With all of the concentration he possessed, Scars thrust his spear into the water awkwardly.

Ramses looked on in anticipation.

Scars grinned proudly as he slowly pulled his spear from the water. His spear bent from the weight of whatever was on the end of it. He lifted the entire spear out of the water excitedly and saw that all he had caught was a large bundle of kelp. Frustrated, Scars threw his spear back into the water and walked away from it angrily. Ramses laughed as he pointed mockingly at his non-fishing friend.

Scars used a piece of wood from the wreckage of the *Carolina Gold* to dig the deeply embedded longboat out of the sand. Still frustrated about his failed attempt at fishing, he dug rapidly.

Ramses soon joined him with three more fish on his spear. He looked down at his frustrated friend and smiled before laying his spear against the boat. He scanned the ground and found another piece of wood. Ramses slowly knelt on the opposite side of the longboat and dug while wearing a satisfied grin. He peeked over the boat at Scars playfully.

Sensing Ramses gaze, Scars continued to dig as he too glanced over the boat. Both of them simultaneously burst into uncontrollable laughter at the day's events.

Later that week, Ramses and Scars sailed on a canal in the longboat they'd reclaimed from the sand of the island. They had fashioned a sail out of a tattered section of sail that had washed up a few days before. They used a thick section of wood they used for a small mast to attach the sail to in the center of their boat.

Scars practiced steering the small vessel by twisting the sail from one side of the makeshift mast to the other. Ramses studied his movements and concentrated intently on Scars' instructions, as he watched how Scars changed the direction of the boat by the subtle movement of its sail. After a few hours of demonstration, Ramses and Scars switched places.

Scars continued to instruct him on the small nuances of sailing as Ramses tried his hand at manipulating the sail. Scars marveled at how quickly Ramses understood and was able to put into action every bit of information he'd shared with him. It was as if Ramses had been born of the sea.

Later that same day, Scars walked up the beach in deep thought. On his stroll, he spied more debris from the wreckage that had washed up. He meandered over to it and began to sift through the tattered remnants of clothing and worn sails, until he came upon a few books from Captain Fletcher's collection. He excitedly picked the books up and ran back down the beach toward their encampment, but suddenly came to an abrupt stop. Scars could not believe his eyes. For strewn over the better part of the beach were literally hundreds of books from Captain Fletcher's collection.

Later that evening, a large campfire burned and crackled illuminating the compound as a cool breeze blew in off the ocean, blowing bright little ambers into the air.

Amidst the semi-completed site of their compound, Ramses sat with his back against a finished section of wall staring stupefied into the large campfire. His eyes looked heavy, as he squinted like he was sleepy.

Scars read to him from a large leather bound book he'd found earlier. He held the book close to his face as he struggled to focus. Ramses slowly turned his head toward Scars.

"Sca, Scars? What do you call this wonderful

beverage?" he muttered.

Scars was visibly inebriated. He dropped the book into the sand and lifted a bottle of rum that was a quarter full to his lips and took a long gulp, then wiped his mouth with his left arm before he answered Ramses' query.

"Rum! It's called rum! The most wonderful creation man ever invented, my friend!" he replied with slurred speech before falling backward into the sand and instantly began to snore.

Ramses lifted the half of a coconut shell he was drinking from up in the direction of the passed out Scars. "Well, my friend, it is very good...!"

The distant sound of a ship's bell interrupted him. At first, Ramses thought it to be the effects of the rum. But when he heard the bell again, he stood immediately and looked out to sea.

Ramses stood, wobbly, and peered into the darkness while walking toward the beach. He could hardly believe his eyes. A schooner sailed past the island only a few miles from shore.

Ramses could see crewmen climbing the main mast and moving about the deck. Their silhouettes could be seen from the light provided by huge candelabrums surrounding the people seated at a large table on the ship's deck. He saw the familiar Spanish flag fluttering in the wind atop the mast as well.

The well-dressed passengers toasted with ornate, solid gold, goblets as the wind blew the scent of butter roasted pig and chicken across the water and into Ramses' keen nostrils. His stomach growled as he imagined how good the delicacies they were enjoying would taste in his own mouth.

Spanish noblemen and women sang a festive song in Spanish while they dined at the lavish table, as multiple servants waited on them.

Ramses continued to watch the schooner until it disappeared over the horizon. He began to formulate a plan as he slowly sat in the sand and pondered his next course of action.

CHAPTER 22

BIRTH OF A PIRATE

Ramses and Scars laid in the longboat floating helplessly in the Gulf of Mexico. The boat rocked from side the side in the current. Both of them seemed close to death as they baked in the unmerciful sunrays without the companion of shade of any kind.

The portly captain of the Spanish ship, that had passed a few days earlier, peered through his long brass spyglass. He had a thick, black mustache with the ends twisted and curled. As he scanned the horizon, he stopped when he noticed the longboat floating aimlessly in the water. He was bound by the Mariners Creed, which dictated that he and his men must attempt to assist any vessel in distress.

Quickly, he collapsed the spyglass on itself and turned to the crewman at the ship's wheel.

"We will see if there are any survivors. Set a course to intercept! Rapido!" he ordered in

Castilian.

The sailor at the helm immediately spun the ship's wheel, steering the massive vessel towards the rocking longboat of Ramses and Scars.

The passengers on the ship, noblemen and women, rushed over to the rail and gawked at the two shipwrecked men. They whispered to one another and pointed at Ramses and Scars who still lay motionless in the longboat.

As the ship pulled alongside the small craft, two sailors hooked the side of it with hooked tipped poles and pulled it close to the side of the ship. The captain looked down into the longboat, seeing if there was any sign of life.

Suddenly, Ramses lifted his hand into the air weakly to let the sailors know he was still alive. The passengers gasped at his display of life. They all found it stimulatingly adventurous. The captain barked more orders to the sailors who had hooked the boat.

"Hurry! Drop the rope ladder! Quickly now!"

The two sailors quickly threw the thick rope ladder over the rail, then as fast as they could, climbed down to assist Ramses and Scars. Once at the bottom, the two of them jumped into the boat.

One of the sailors carefully and gently rolled Ramses onto his back as not to injure him in his weakened state. Much to his surprise, Ramses rolled over holding both of his custom shotgun pistols, which he cocked both hammers at the same time and held on both the startled sailors. Scars rolled over and cocked his pistol as well. He pointed it at the other sailor's face and grinned playfully. The two sailors raised their hands into the air and looked up helplessly and confused at their captain.

The captain looked down into the boat trying to understand what was happening. Ramses motioned to the two sailors with his pistols trained on them to climb back up the rope ladder. Scars held his pistol on the many stunned bystanders at the rail of the ship as Ramses and the sailors scaled the ladder. Once at the top, he jumped down onto the deck fearlessly.

The nobles all gasped at the fierceness and sheer size of Ramses. Scars followed closely behind, then he too jumped down onto the deck of the Spanish ship. Ramses kept the pistol in his left hand at his captors and pointed to the deck with the pistol in his right.

"You will form a line here, quickly now!" he authoritatively ordered with his deep voice.

Everyone, from the sailors to the nobles, complied rapidly and made their way in front of Ramses and Scars to form a line. The passengers, sailors and captain stood in a line facing Ramses and Scars. Ramses continued to hold his custom pistols on them as he kept his eyes trained on them for any aggressive movements of any kind.

Scars enjoyed his new line of work. He walked down the line of people, stopping periodically to view the many baubles and trinkets the noblemen and women had in their possession. In his hands he carried a large burlap sack, which the people dropped their valuables into as he passed. He stopped in front of a beautiful noblewoman who tried to cover her diamond necklace with her hand.

Scars smirked at her as he reached out to take the necklace. The woman chided him in English with a heavy Spanish accent.

"This necklace has been in my family for four

generations!"

An overweight nobleman standing next to the noblewoman stepped out of the group and protested vigorously.

"If you two bandits know what is good for you, you will leave this ship at once... or my father will hunt the both of you down like the stinking coweredly dogs you are!"

Ramses walked toward the defiant nobleman slow and calm, then without warning clubbed him on the bridge of his nose with the butt of the shotgun pistol in his right hand.

The nobleman fell to the deck clutching his nose whimpering and crying as blood gushed from both nostrils of his broken nose. Ramses, emotionless, slowly backed away from the line and retrained his pistols on the people. Scars turned slightly and watched as the overweight nobleman writhed in pain. He turned back and looked into the face of the noblewoman.

"Now then, do you think he feels better or worse?" he asked in a calm and sarcastic tone before he reached out and snatched the necklace from her throat and placed the item into the bag.

The woman yelled at him in anger. "Sir, you

are not a gentleman! I am of noble blood!"

Scars turned again and faced the woman aggressively. "You are absalutely correct. I am not a gentleman! So get your ass back into line before I slap your noble ass over that rail!" he yelled, before bowing to her mockingly. "Madame."

The noblewoman immediately stopped speaking and lowered her head as she took her place again in line once more.

Ramses studied the ship. He saw the sails flapping in the wind and the many ropes and large wooden pulleys connected to the main mast. His ears tuned in to the seagulls squawking nervously overhead as they spread their wings and hovered on the warm jet streams. Slowly, he turned and locked his eyes on the ship's wheel.

Scars ran over to Ramses with his bag of booty excited.

"There must be a couple thousand dollars worth of shit in this bag! Not bad for a day's work, huh, Cap? You know, we may be on to something with this piracy thing," he concluded while holding the sack open in front of Ramses.

Oblivious to what Scars was talking about,

Ramses looked at him.

"How many men would it take to man a vessel such as this?"

Scars stopped shaking the bag of loot for a moment and stared at Ramses confused.

"Uh, I don't know, maybe 10 or 20. I mean, if they are experienced sailors, we could do it with less. Why do you ask?"

Ramses smirked a little as he turned and stared menacingly at the chubby Spanish captain, his sailors and the noble passengers. He then turned and gave a head gesture to Scars. Scars, finally realizing what Ramses was implying, laughed hysterically.

Less than an hour later, the portly captain and every other soul that was on his ship were crammed in the longboat that Ramses and Scars had arrived in. He sat in the bow of the boat dejected and sad as he watched his own ship sail away.

Ramses stood proudly on the helm of his newly acquired vessel in front of the wheel. He scanned around the ship admiring it. Scars stood at the ship's rail and waved goodbye mockingly to the Spanish captain and his passengers. He rubbed a shiny red apple on his left shirtsleeve, then took a bite of it. He chewed and laughed as he walked over to Ramses.

"Well... uh... Captain Ramses, what will be your first official order? Uh... sir," he asked with a sarcastic tone, while trying to keep a straight face.

Ramses turned to him with determination in his eyes.

"Now, we make the ships that pass our island... pay for the privilege," he replied confidently before breaking into a sinister smile.

Scars tossed the apple overboard and grabbed his belly, as he laughed hardily.

"Oh, that is good! Oh, that is quite good!"

CHAPTER 23

THE SOCIETY

Fulani sat inside a circular, wooden tub deep in her own thoughts. Wisps of steam from the hot water wafted into the air. Naira gently dipped a piece of cloth into the water of the bath, then squeezed the excess water from it before placing the rag onto Fulani's naked back. She wiped the princess' back gently.

"Princess, where did you learn to fight like that? You are a great warrior. Did your father teach you the art of battle? I predict you shall win many battles inside the pit."

She wiped down the center of Fulani's back before turning and dipping the rag into the water once more. Fulani lowered her head for a moment, then lifted it before answering.

"It was not my father, but my mother, the warrior-queen Sumitra, who trained me in the art of battle. Since the time I was able to hold a sickle knife in my hand, she instructed and tested me, as was the custom of her tribe, the Limbikani. As it will be with my daughter as well."

Fulani touched her belly gently with her right hand.

Naira interrupted.

"Oh, the Limbikani, I have heard legends about them from the elders of my village! Is it true that the men do the cooking and rear the children, while the women of the tribe hunt and train for battle?"

Fulani sighed before she answered.

"Yes, it is true."

"That is so exciting! The women of my village just cooked and cleaned and produced babies. You are very lucky to have been raised in the ways of battle," rebutted Naira, still excited to know that for once the legend she had been told was true.

Fulani remembered something that Naira had mentioned in their conversation earlier that peaked her interest. She turned her head slightly and asked, "The pit? What is this pit you spoke of? Has the Brazilian fought in this pit?"

Naira was overwhelmed by the rapidness of

Fulani's queries.

"Princess, slow down," she giggled. "One question at a time. My Ashante is good but not that good. I shall have to teach you to speak the language of our captors."

Fulani smiled briefly, then stopped as Naira continued.

"There is more than one pit. They are large deep holes dug into the earth near the plantations of members of a secret group simply known as *The Society.*

"*The Society* is made up of some of the richest and most powerful men in the South. Captain Bishop is one of its founding members. This is the reason for your abduction, my Princess. The men in *The Society* enjoy watching women warriors do battle in the pits, as well as men. Sometimes, they order them to fight to the death. These men I speak of are twisted and vile creatures. Once a month they hold what they call tournaments, where the members wager large amounts of gold, silver and sometimes slaves on who they think will win these battles."

Fulani hung on Naira's every word.

Naira dipped the rag into the water again,

turned and moved from the princess' back to her left side. She lifted Fulani's arm and began to wipe it with the rag before continuing her story. "The fights are only one of the many exotic attractions found at these private tournaments."

Fulani raised her eyebrows quizzically.

"What else do these men do?" she asked, eager to hear Naira's answer.

"At these tournaments the members of *The Society* indulge in every type of perversion they can think of, with slaves, white women, and dare I say... each other!"

Both of them laughed into their hands like schoolgirls before being startled by an unwelcome visitor, as the cabin door swung open.

The Brazilian stepped into the room scowling. She held the black sarong she wore in front with both hands, as she glared menacingly at the two women suspiciously. In her heavy Spanish accent she addressed them.

"What are you two laughing about? Do you not see where you are? You laugh because you have no idea of where you are being taken or what will be done to you once you get there!"

Fulani stood and glared angrily at Carlota.

Carlota glared back defiantly.

"If you do not wish to swim with the sharks, I suggest we keep things civil, until it is time for me to kill you."

Naira translated to Fulani rapidly.

Fulani stood there peering at Carlota.

Carlota stood defiant, peering back at Fulani.

After a few tense seconds Fulani smirked at Carlota and sat back down.

Carlota walked around the tub toward where Fulani and Naira were. She dipped her left hand into the water to test how hot it was and flicked some of it into the air. Once she was in front of Fulani she allowed her sarong to fall to the floor, revealing her curvaceous cocoa brown body and smooth, shaven pelvic area.

"And if you behave yourself, Princess, I will let you taste something so sweet that you will not have any need for a man again!"

Carlota deliberately stepped over Fulani's head with her womanhood within inches of her face. Once inside the tub, the Brazilian lowered herself into it and playfully flicked the water at the blushing Naira.

Fulani scoffed, stood and turned to face the relaxed Carlota.

"If you ever put that foul thing near me again, I will bite it off and spit it into your face!" The princess stormed out as Naira translated what she said to Carlota.

Carlota smirked, unphased by Fulani's threat and submerged her head underneath the steaming bath water.

Naira quickly grabbed the sheer sarong that Fulani had left in the bath cabin and caught up with her as she entered her quarters.

"Uhhh, I have never wanted to end someone's life as badly as I want to end hers!" screamed Fulani.

Naira timidly approached the princess with the sarong.

"Princess, please cover yourself before you catch your death," implored Naira, as she cautiously approached the angry princess.

Fulani calmed herself and nodded to Naira. She took the sarong from the young girl's tiny hands and placed it around herself.

Suddenly, there was an unexpected knock on the cabin door before a large crewman entered.

"I am to take you to Captain Bishop's quarters now."

"What for?" asked Fulani in Ashanti.

Naira asked in English. "The princess demands to know what for?"

The crewman pulled the belaying pin from his belt with his right hand and stepped aggressively toward Fulani. Fulani put her fists up and prepared to fight. Naira acted quickly.

"Alright, alright, she will come. You do not have to force her!"

The crewman stopped and glared at the defiant Fulani. He looked her up and down lustfully, as the candlelight behind her made her sarong see through.

"Yep, the captain sure can pick 'em."

He pointed the belaying pin near Naira's face.

"Now, you get this bitch to the Captain's quarters immediately or I'll come back here and ass rape both of you," he chuckled, took another glance at Fulani, then left.

Naira turned to Fulani who still had her fists raised in front of her.

"We must go to the captain's quarters, my Princess. Prepare yourself for anything, for he is without honor."

Fulani reluctantly agreed as she lowered her hands to her sides dejected.

Naira placed Fulani's hands gently into hers and led her out of the cabin door.

When they arrived outside of Captain Bishop's cabin door an uneasy feeling came over Fulani. A cold chill ran down her spine and her heart beat rapidly in her chest.

Two sizable guards were posted outside of his quarters on opposite sides of the entrance. Both men ignored Fulani and Naira as they cautiously entered the cabin. Inside, the captain's quarters was brightly illuminated with ornate iron candelabras, too many to count. The room was filled with candle smoke.

Fulani smelled a familiar scent emanating in the captain's cabin. She remembered the fragrance from the night that she and the Mortisi were ambushed and taken. *Opium,* she assumed.

In that moment, the princess relived the painful details of that ill-fated night, in an instant. She relived the memory of the last time she'd laid eyes on her beloved Bambara as she left the ship with her brother that night. Her eyes began to well up. She quickly tried to compose herself as not to give Captain Bishop the satisfaction of seeing her cry.

Fulani and Naira walked toward the captain. They stopped only a few feet away from where he was sitting, wearing a blue silk robe that was open.

Captain Bishop sat behind his huge table in front of his charts. His eyes were sleepy and he was very calm, as he sat back in his ornate, leather bound chair with a high back. A sizable carafe of wine sat on the table in front of him. He poured some wine into a beautifully crafted golden goblet, then lifted it toward Fulani.

"Well hello! I was afraid that I was going to have to send some of my men to escort you here, Princess."

Naira translated to Fulani.

Fulani scoffed and rolled her eyes at him.

Captain Bishop shrugged his shoulders and drank from the goblet. He placed it back onto the table then spoke.

"We will be arriving at my plantation soon. There will be certain duties that I need to know you will perform, without complaint."

Naira translated the captain's last statement.

Fulani glared at him suspiciously.

"And what are these duties you speak of?" asked the princess in Ashanti. Naira echoed her query in English to the captain.

Captain Bishop seemed to be preoccupied. He paused briefly and let out a quick moan before he answered.

Both women were curious about his behavior. He laughed loudly, clapped his hands, then stood and revealed his nakedness from the waist down. His pale, thick manhood was erect and throbbing.

Naira shielded her eyes with her left hand.

A few moments after, Carlota climbed from under the table. She glanced at Fulani provocatively as she wiped the saliva from her mouth with her right hand. Her sarong was open in front and hugged the sides of her perfect breasts. She kept her eyes on Fulani and Naira as she slowly climbed onto the table and put her buttocks in the air facing Captain Bishop on all fours. Carlota lifted her right hand off the table and with her pointer finger, signaled Fulani to join her.

Fulani scoffed defiantly and abruptly turned to leave the room.

Captain Bishop unphased, placed both hands on either side of Carlota's voluptuous buttocks and spread it apart. Before he sank his face into it, he glared at Fulani at the door menacingly.

"Either you will do my bidding...or maybe your companion, young Lisa, would have to take your place? Maybe I should recant our agreement from earlier and put that nigger bastard you carry in your belly into the fields in its fourth year of life!" he yelled threateningly.

Naira translated loudly to Fulani.

Fulani halted at the cabin door and cringed at the thought of Captain Bishop defiling Naira or her unborn child sentenced to a life of mundane toil in the fields. Slowly, she turned back around and returned to Naira's side. Fulani turned to her. "You must go."

Naira looked into Fulani's face.

"I will not leave you, Princess. Your fate will be my fate."

Fulani grabbed her by the shoulders.

"Do you serve me?"

"Yes, Princess. In all things."

Fulani looked deeply into the young girl's eyes.

"Then, serve me now! Leave this room!" she implored her young friend.

Captain Bishop buried his head into Carlota's bottom and slurped loudly.

Fulani became impatient with Naira's defiance. She grabbed her by the arm and forced her out of the captain's cabin and slammed the door behind her. Fulani looked up as she leaned against the cabin door. Finally, she made the decision to surrender herself for Naira, her unborn child and her own survival.

Slowly, she began to remove her sarong and allowed it to fall to the floor. She walked toward the awaiting Carlota.

Carlota grinned seductively as she again signaled for Fulani to come to her. Fulani silently prayed for strength, as the Brazilian began to kiss her belly softly. She tensed up, clinched her fists and held both arms out to her sides. Carlota gripped Fulani's taught buttocks and pulled her vagina as close as she could to her face. She began to explore Fulani's womanhood with the tip of her tongue. The princess tried desperately to think of Bambara to ease the shame, but to no avail.

Captain Bishop licked and prodded Carlota's butt with his tongue.

She moaned and reared back on his face as she simultaneously pleasured Fulani orally.

Fulani tried as hard as she could not to enjoy the experience, but the Brazilian was a skilled lover. Before the princess realized what was happening, she grabbed Carlota by the back of the head with both hands, placed her right foot up on the table and ground her pelvis into the Brazilian's mouth.

Sensing that Fulani was nearing climax, Carlota removed her right hand from Fulani's ass and jabbed two fingers into Fulani's vagina, rapidly, as she slid her tongue from side to side quickly, while she growled like an animal.

Fulani, now caught up in the throngs of sexual fervor threw her head back and thrust her womanhood onto Carlota's fingers and mouth, violently. Her breathing became heavier as she gushed to climax all over the face and hand of her perceived enemy.

Captain Bishop lifted his head and smiled. He

pulled his head out of Carlota's privates and turned. The captain picked up the opium pipe off of his chart shelf. He walked around the table and stood behind the still climaxing Fulani and placed the pipe up to her mouth. He grabbed a candle from his table and held the flame to the pipe. Fulani puffed gently twice and the effects of the opium took her over immediately. Captain Bishop smiled, grabbed her left breast and kissed Fulani's neck.

"Oh, I have some special things planned for you, my beauty. As long as you serve me, you will have whatever you need. But betray me... and you and yours will be put to the blade!"

Fulani was disoriented.

The Brazilian lifted her face from Fulani's womanhood with a wide grin.

Captain Bishop pushed Fulani face first onto his table. He spit in his right hand and wiped it on the throbbing head of his penis, then without warning, forced his thick manhood deep into Fulani's rectum. Fulani screamed in agony so loudly that it echoed through the halls of the ship for all to hear.

Naira sat by herself in a dark corner below

decks and cried uncontrollably. When she heard Fulani's screams, she fell deeper into sadness and sobbed for the pain she imagined Fulani must now endure.

CHAPTER 24

EVERYDAY

On the caye, Ramses and Scars walked down a narrow sandy path cut through a dense mangrove forest. Scars carried two large burlap sacks over his well-defined shoulders. Ramses' arms were filled with six muskets and multiple gunpowder horns were draped about his neck.

Both men stopped in front of a huge naturally hollowed out tree, which stood in the very center of the mangroves at the end of the trail. Ramses placed the muskets into the hollow of tree, then removed the powder horns from his neck and placed them inside the tree as well.

Scars dropped the two burlap sacks into the tree. The jingle of coins and other precious metal objects could be heard when the overstuffed sacks made contact with the ground. Ramses turned his head to Scars excitedly.

"Just think of it, this is only the beginning!"

A few months later, Ramses and Scars

walked down the same narrow path with more sacks of stolen gold in their possession. Once at the tree, they both realized that there was no more room left in it to place another item. They both forced the new sacks into the spaceless tree. The sacks held for a few moments before tumbling out and spilling hundreds of Spanish gold coins onto the sand.

Ramses and Scars looked down at all of the gold and silver they had amassed in such a short period of time. They lifted their heads simultaneously, turned to one another, shrugged their shoulders and nonchalantly walked away giggling.

The construction of their stronghold was complete. The walls of the main structure were high and secure with armed members of their crew posted on each corner of it. Also on the wall were four large, thick, black, iron cannons pointed towards the bay. The men on guard duty craned their heads left and right as they kept an eagle eye on the calm open sea.

A big, bright full super moon hung low in the sky over the calm waters and the sound of cheerful guitar music emanated from inside the completed stronghold.

Inside its high wooden walls, a scantily clad raven-haired woman, wearing a red scarf wrapped around her head, dipped a large wooden cup into a barrel of beer. Once her goblet was full, she turned and walked with it over to Ramses. The woman lifted the cup over his head.

Ramses wobbled a bit as he tilted his head back as far as it would go, then opened his mouth wide. The raven-haired woman poured the contents into his mouth in a slow steady stream. Liquid spilled from the sides of Ramses' mouth.

The raven-haired woman stood on the tips of her toes, opened her mouth wide and attempted to catch the spillage from his mouth into her own mouth. She continued to pour until the cup was totally empty.

The ethnically diverse men and women who surrounded the campfire responded to Ramses' sloppy attempt to consume the contents of the cup. They jeered him and lifted their own cups and jugs into the air and mocked him playfully.

Ramses was totally inebriated. The solid gold crown upon his head was cocked to the side and the beautiful silk robe he wore flailed in the wind behind him. His left arm he kept around the strong, shapely shoulders of a voluptuous African girl and he had a similarly endowed dark-haired Spanish beauty to his right, as he gulped the contents of the sexy raven-haired girl's goblet.

Once finished, he raised his arms in a victory-like fashion. Ramses wiped the remnants of the beer off his face with his right hand, then grabbed the raven-haired girl by the face and pulled it to his. His tongue darted and swirled around in her mouth as he kissed her passionately.

Suddenly, the African girl and other Spanish girl grabbed the raven-haired woman by the hair. They began to pull hair, scratch, bite and wrestle each other until all of them fell to the ground. The others around the fire cheered them on vigorously.

Scars came out of the cabin with the front of his pants open, his shirt partially hung off of his left shoulder. He stopped in the doorway, turned back and blew a kiss to the three women lying naked on the sandy floor of the cabin. He turned once more and walked over to the campfire and bowed stylishly to Ramses.

Scars was wearing a large, fancy, blue, Spanish-style wide brim hat, complete with a long feather on the right side of it. He wrapped himself in a delicate embroidered robe and had gold and diamond rings on every finger of both hands. Scars smiled widely as he produced a silver flask from beneath the robe and took an elongated swig. Once done, he laughed with Ramses as they watched the three women-wrestling match. Scars passed the flask to Ramses.

Ramses lifted the flask and toasted to Scars and took a long swig. He scrunched his face from the burn of the whiskey and passed it back to Scars. Ramses shook his head rapidly, as he tried to shake off some of the effects of the alcohol, then walked over to a large wooden chest sitting in the sand next to the wall of the compound.

Once there, he opened it and revealed gold and jewels of all shapes and sizes. Ramses dug his hands into the jewels and coins and lifted them in both hands, as if he were bathing in them. He turned to Scars and spoke without a hint of his former African accent, but slurred his words drunkenly.

"We haven't done bad for ourselves... these past years... have we? How long has it been, my friend? I find myself losing track of time."

Scars squinted at Ramses as he tried to focus. He walked carefully toward the chest, turned and sat in the sand with his back against it, then took another drink from his flask before answering Ramses.

"Nope! Not bad at all for a couple of... for a couple of... runaway slaves," he slurred then burped loudly and continued.

"According to my drunken calculations... you and I have been in this line of employment for..." He lifted his left hand and closed his left eye as he tried once more to focus. Scars put his pinky finger down, then the finger next to it.

"Uuuuh... about two years?"

Scars chuckled then drank a long, slow swig. He looked up at the glowing full moon and became a bit serious. "Do you still think about her?"

Ramses frowned his face quizzically.

"Think about who?"

Scars became visibly upset. He threw the flask into the sand and stood up straight, trying to keep his balance in the process.

" *'Who'*... he says!"

Scars pointed at Ramses' feet, insulted that Ramses even had to ask.

"Your feet don't grab branches, Captain! *'Who?'* Fulani, that's who!"

Ramses became angry. He scoffed and walked quickly away from Scars and the others up the narrow path toward the hollowed out tree. He sat in the sand and placed his back against the tree. Ramses sighed deeply as he raised his head and stared at the super moon. Under his breath he responded to Scars' query earlier.

"Everyday."

CHAPTER 25

WARRIOR MOTHER

Fulani looked into the sky studying the same full super moon that Ramses was looking up into that same night. She wore a black robe with a large hood over her head. An indistinct murmur of a large group of people talking traveled through the air around the sprawling Bishop Plantation.

Fulani dropped to her knees, lifted her palms to the sky, bowed her head and closed her eyes to pray.

"Oh Mighty Nyame, creator of the three realms, hear me now. I, Fulani, Princess of the Ashanti, daughter of the mighty Chief Yoruba and your humble servant, implore you to make me swift... make me strong... and please, I beg of you, to keep me alive long enough to take revenge on my oppressors! To you, Omnipotent One... I pray."

Suddenly, the two large wooden doors behind

her opened. The light of many torches hit Fulani's back as she remained on her knees. A smiling Captain Bishop entered the room and spoke definitively.

"It's time."

Fulani stood slowly. She turned and walked passed the captain into a circular earthen fighting pit. The crowd of spectators, dressed in colonial attire, seated around the top of the pit, watched Fulani as she entered. She entered the pit slow and proud with her head raised high and confident.

There was a carnival like atmosphere around the pit. Blood splatter and chunks of flesh stained the walls of the fighting pit from prior spectacles. The red clay and dirt floor of the pit was strewn with puddles of dried and fresh blood.

The spectators were men of wealth, whose every whim was satisfied by an assorted array of slaves, male and female, who plied them with whiskey and wine during the bouts. When the mob saw Fulani enter the pit, the audience went wild in anticipation of the next fight.

Many of the plantation owners waved money

or pouches of gold over their heads to gain the attention of a slender and seedy looking gentleman with wads of paper money between the fingers of his left hand. He grabbed money from three of the men waving it as fast as he could before Fulani's fight started.

Fulani could smell the stench of dried blood and death within the pit. She concentrated on staying calm and controlling her nerves as she breathed. She could feel her heart pound in her chest.

A few moments after she entered the pit, Captain Bishop entered wearing a white suit with a top hat that matched. In his right hand, he carried a black walking stick with a silver knight on the head of it. He walked around Fulani, as he played up to the crowd, before he made his way to the center of the pit and raised his arms, silencing them. Slowly, the crowd hushed.

Captain Bishop spoke as if he were a carnival barker. "Ladies and the rest of y'all," the crowd laughed as he continued.

"It is my distinct pleasure to bring to you the main scrap of the evening! I have behind me the one you came to see! I found her in the jungles of West Africa! I brought her to this land to become *The Society's* fighting slave champion, and you know what? She is," he chuckled.

"So, without any further adieu, I give to you... the beautiful, the deadly... Blaaaaaack Naaaaaancy!" Captain Bishop swung his hand around in the direction of Black Nancy.

Black Nancy removed her hood and allowed her robe to fall to the ground. She wore a very revealing leather X-shaped harness, which barely covered her ample breasts. The handles of her sickles were to either side of her shaven head. Her body was in incredible condition, every muscle was flexed and easy to see. The torchlight reflected off her perfectly smooth dark skin. She turned toward the doors of the pit and stared into the darkness behind them and waited in deadly anticipation.

The crowd was abuzz with expectation and cheered wildly. An overweight plantation owner licked his tongue out suggestively toward Black Nancy and shouted, "Show us what you're made of, Darky, and I'll show you what I'm made of later!"

While yet another member sodomized a

young slave girl from behind as she gripped the side of the wooden planks that lined the walls of the pit. She moaned loudly as she forced herself back onto him repeatedly.

A different slave girl performed fellatio on a plantation owner in the front row. He grabbed the back of her head and pressed it down harder onto his penis before climaxing violently into the back of her throat.

"I hope that you've all placed your bets," announced Captain Bishop.

The seedy man taking the bets nodded to the captain, signaling to him that all of the bets were in.

Captain Bishop nodded back.

"Tonight's contest will be *The Society's* first ever handicapped match! What is a handicapped match, you ask? Well, let me clarify for you bunch of degenerates! Black Nancy will fight not one, but two opponents tonight, at once!"

The spectators began to murmur excitedly. Captain Bishop raised his arms once again to quiet the crowd.

"Black Nancy is the only undefeated champion *The Society* has ever had! Will her luck run out tonight? We shall see!"

He turned back towards the large doors at the entrance of the pit. Two young, male slaves jumped into the pit and ran over to the doors, slowly opening them, revealing nothing but darkness on the other side.

Captain Bishop backed away slowly from the center of the fighting area. He spun around quickly and made his way to the wooden ladder fastened to the wall of the pit and climbed up, then stood on the front row at the wall.

A slave girl with huge, perky breasts immediately walked over to him and handed the captain a goblet filled with drink. She reached down in the waist of her skirt and pulled a cigar from it and placed it into his mouth. She struck a wooden match against the wall of the pit and lit his cigar.

Captain Bishop puffed a few times on the cigar and twisted it to ignite it properly. Once lit, he took the drink in his right hand and drank it straight down with no hesitation, then slammed the empty goblet down on the top of the wall. He turned to the spectators and grinned slyly as he lifted his right hand into the air to start the contest.

"Begin!"

Without warning, two massive male slaves ran out-- muscles bulging. Both of them ran into the pit yelling wildly. One entered carrying an axe with dried blood on its blade. The other wielded a spear with a long-notched, bloody tip.

The men circled Black Nancy, cautiously as they slowly tightened the amount of space between them and her.

Black Nancy stood calmly in the center of the pit. The only thing she moved were her eyes, as she kept them trained on the men circling her.

Suddenly, the slave with the spear attacked. He jabbed at her head with his spear. Black Nancy skillfully moved only her head from one side to the other and made him miss. The slave wielding the spear attempted to bring his weapon across her head. Black Nancy ducked her head as the spear swept over her. She could hear it cutting through the wind.

Frustrated, the slave with the spear yelled as he regrouped. He skillfully twirled his spear in his hands as he stalked Black Nancy. After a few tense moments he attacked once again, this time at her feet. He jabbed at her legs and feet with the tip of the spear.

Black Nancy, with catlike agility, moved her feet up, then down and back and forth, avoiding the tip of her challenger's spear. The spearman swung it around his head and attempted to take Black Nancy's legs out with a powerful sweep.

Simultaneously, the slave wielding the axe attacked Nancy. He bellowed a war cry and swung the axe with all his strength.

Black Nancy jumped high into the air. She brought her knees into her chest to raise her feet all in one motion. The slave with the spear just missed her legs by inches.

Nancy brought her feet back to the ground swiftly and bent backward like a contortionist. She placed her palms on the ground to support her position and barely avoided the other slave's axe, which missed connecting with her abdomen by less than an inch.

The fighting slave with the axe and the other with the spear glanced at one another a bit confused.

Black Nancy brought her body upright again. She glared at her opponents and smirked defiantly.

"My turn," she said in perfect English, without a hint of an African accent.

Black Nancy reached behind her head and pulled her sickles from their harness. She extended both arms out to her sides. The torchlight reflected off the two polished blades of her sickles as she began to twirl them stylishly over her head, then behind her back, then side to side.

The members of *The Society* marveled at her mastery and applauded excitedly.

She twirled the sickles in front of her once more before allowing the leather straps at the bottom of the sickles to become wrapped around her hands tightly. Black Nancy glanced over at her two opponents and winked her right eye at them, calm and defiant. Then she opened her right hand and motioned her fingers back and forth, coaxing the two fighters to come for her.

The two slave fighters turned slightly and glanced at one another unsure. They turned their heads slowly back towards Black Nancy. Both men nodded, then simultaneously attacked her with fierce determination.

The fighting slave wielding the spear jabbed at her repeatedly as the other swung his axe with deadly intent.

The princess backed up slowly as she blocked the spear and the axe. Sparks flew each time she blocked their weapons with her sickles. She'd block to one side, then, the other.

The slave fighter with the axe swung it at Black Nancy's head. She instinctively crossed her sickles in front of her face and blocked the axe just before it struck her in the head.

The slave with the spear saw an opening and jabbed Black Nancy in the side with the tip of his spear, piercing her in the ribs on her left side.

Black Nancy pushed the axe away, jumped to the right, tumbled over and jumped back to her feet. She touched the wound in her side. Slowly, she lifted her hand and saw it covered in blood. She glared at the two fighting slaves with even more determination than before. The princess twirled her sickles once more.

The two fighters looked at Nancy's wounded side. The slave with the axe motioned to the slave with the spear with his head to attack her again.

Black Nancy stood at the ready with her sickles poised in the direction of the two fighters.

The slave fighter with the spear took a deep breath, then snapped the spear down into attack position in front of him. He paused for a moment, then ran toward Black Nancy yelling like a madman.

Black Nancy blocked the lunging spear with the sickle in her left hand and spun swinging the sickle in her right hand as she did so, cutting off both the spearman's arms just below his elbows. Before his spear hit the ground, she caught it on top of her right foot and flipped it back into the air. Then in one swift motion grabbed the spear out of the air with her right hand, with the spearman's severed hands still clutching its shaft, spun once more and threw the spear at the fighting slave with the axe with all the strength she could muster.

The spear hit its mark, striking the axeman in his mouth and through the back of his head. His eyes widened and his facial expression was one of astonishment.

The now silent crowd could hear an

unpleasant gurgling sound emanating from the axeman's mouth, as he fell backwards to the dusty ground with the spear sticking out of his face and the hands and forearms of the spearman still clutching the spear's shaft.

Captain Bishop jumped to his feet, as well as the other *Society* members in attendance and applauded frantically, for never had they seen anyone remotely close to the prowess of the princess.

Black Nancy twirled the leather strap on the sickle in her right hand again. She turned slowly toward the fallen warrior with the spear.

He wriggled on the ground whimpering in pain as his heart continued to pump blood through his body, which wound up in a puddle on the ground leaking from his arm stubs. He turned his head in the direction of Black Nancy. She walked toward him slowly.

The spectators began to clap melodically with each step Black Nancy took toward the downed spearman.

The spearman rolled over and attempted to crawl away from her using only his feet and elbows until the wooden-lined wall of the pit stopped him. He turned to the oncoming princess.

"Please, don't kill me," he begged.

Black Nancy continued to walk slowly toward him. Once there, she stood over the spearman with tears in her eyes.

"You do not understand, brother. We are all already dead. May Nyame welcome you!"

The princess lifted the sickle in her right hand, then, in one compact motion, swung and lopped the spearman's head from his shoulders. Blood gushed from his headless body, as Black Nancy spun away from him.

Captain Bishop and all of the other spectators began to applaud wildly!

Black Nancy threw her sickles to the ground in disgust as she walked across the blood soaked pit. She passed the body of the axeman and made her way through the large doors that she had entered through earlier.

Outside and visibly distraught, the princess strolled on the grounds of the sprawling Bishop Plantation. The princess continued until she came upon an awaiting group of small slave children who also were captives on the Bishop

Estate.

One of them, a little girl no more than the age of seven, ran up to Black Nancy so excited she could hardly contain herself.

"Miss Nancy, when I get big, I want to be just like you! I want to be a champion in the pits!"

Black Nancy stopped abruptly and looked at the little girl. She began to say something to the girl, but decided to hold her tongue while fighting back tears. Instead, she forced a half smile and gave the girl a token pat on the shoulder and made her way as quick as she could toward a barn across from the main house in the center of the plantation.

Still beside herself with excitement, the little girl watched as Black Nancy disappeared into the barn. She bent down and picked up a small tree branch from the ground and held it tightly in her right hand. The little girl stood, then turned to the other young slave children.

"I'm Black Nancy," she decreed playfully.

The little slave girl then proceeded to pretend the stick was one of Black Nancy's sickles and began to act as if she was slashing the other children with it. The other children playfully fell to the ground as if they had been slain by her.

Black Nancy entered the barn and closed the door behind her. Inside, the walls were lined with stalls for livestock. A few oil lamps that hung on the walls illuminated the barn.

As Black Nancy walked by the stalls, the fighting slaves chained in them stood as a sign of respect to her. They began to clap melodically to honor yet another one of her victories. Finally, she arrived at her own stall and entered.

In her stall, Lisa rocked back and forth as she rocked a female toddler in a simple handmade, wooden cradle and hummed a cheerful African tune.

The princess paused for a moment and watched the touching sight. She approached Lisa and the baby, but was struck with a sharp pain from the wound in her side. Lisa saw her pause in pain.

"Oh Princess, you have been wounded! Please take a seat!"

Black Nancy scoffed. "No, Naira, I will be fine. The wound is only one of the flesh. It will heal quickly when I sew it up."

Lisa just smiled, for it was never guaranteed

that the princess would return from battle in the pits at all.

"You have won yet again. This is good. Nyame has great plans for you. I have seen this in my dreams, Princess."

Black Nancy did not respond. She just continued to stare into the cradle at her daughter. The princess held her arms out to Lisa. Lisa understood exactly what she wanted. She carefully picked the baby girl out of the cradle and handed her to Black Nancy, then as quietly as she could, left the stall.

Black Nancy glared down at her baby girl with motherly love in her eyes. The baby awoke and began to cry.

"Shhhhhh, little one, momma is here now. Shhhhh," she whispered.

The baby girl looked up and saw her mother's face. She immediately stopped crying and smiled. Black Nancy smiled lovingly down at the baby and gently swung her from side to side.

"One day, you and I gonna leave this place, my beautiful Ruby. We are going to find your father, wherever he might be. I promise, baby girl... I promise."

She lifted Ruby up to her lips and kissed her gently on the forehead.

Suddenly, Captain Bishop's drunken voice shattered the tender moment.

"Oh, are you now? Tell me... when will this monumental event be taking place? I would surely like to be there when all of this finding that bastard's father takes place. You know as well as I do... that nigger is pickin' somebody's cotton or sugarcane or even better... he's dead! Why would you want to fill that nigglin's head with all them lies and promises?"

He walked into the stall and put his arms out to hold the child. Black Nancy clutched her baby tighter. Captain Bishop's smirk slowly became a scowl.

"Give me that goddamn gal before I whip the hide off both of you! Do not test me girl, give her here," he said aggressively.

Black Nancy, with arms shaking nervously, complied and passed the toddler to Captain Bishop.

Captain Bishop held the baby girl in his arms gently, rocking her up and down like a proud poppa.

"Please, do not hurt her. She is all I have in this world, Masta Bishop," pleaded the princess.

Captain Bishop scoffed as he lifted his head and glared at Black Nancy offended.

"Why, Nancy, I am deeply saddened that you would even entertain such notions about me. I would not dream of hurting your baby. Hell, we are practically family, aren't we?"

Relieved, Black Nancy relaxed a bit and struggled to put a token smile on her face for the captain.

"I thank you, sir."

Captain Bishop walked the baby over to the cradle and gently placed her back into it. Ruby started to cry loudly. Black Nancy rushed to the cradle to pick the baby up.

Captain Bishop grabbed her arm as she passed him. He peered into Nancy's eyes sinisterly.

"Now, you know what you have to do to make sure that baby stays as healthy as she is now, don't you?"

Black Nancy dropped her head. She lifted it again slowly and sighed. Dejectedly, she looked up at the smirking Captain Bishop, then backed away. The princess unbuckled her harness and allowed it to drop to the floor and revealed her stunningly beautiful and perfectly fit physique.

Captain Bishop walked slowly around Black Nancy studying her body lustfully. He gently ran the fingers of his right hand across her skin as he made his way around her.

Black Nancy cringed in disgust from Captain Bishop's touch. She tried as hard as she could not to show the level of her disdain. He stopped in front of her and dropped his pants abruptly.

Black Nancy looked up at him, then slowly dropped to her knees. A single tear trailed down her left cheek as she descended, which she wiped quickly so that the captain would not see.

Captain Bishop looked down and smiled as the princess performed fellatio on him.

"You are where you belong, and this is where you're gonna stay, my beautiful dark champion, or your daughter will not live to see the age of three!"

The captain gripped the back of her head and ejaculated with a loud animalistic grunt.

CHAPTER 26

A DECADE HAS PASSED

A longboat floated on the currents in the Gulf of Mexico. Two of Ramses' pirates were lying in the bottom of the boat motionless, pretending to be overcome by the intense rays of the summer sun. An English frigate pulled alongside them slowly, then anchored, bringing the vessel to a complete stop. One of Ramses' men lifted his hand to signal the ship that he was still alive, perpetrating the ruse that Ramses himself invented.

A handsome, pale skinned young commanding officer of the frigate glared down at the two men in the longboat. He yelled down to the two men and attempted to stimulate a response from them.

"Ahoy there! My name is Commander Marlowe! Can we offer you chaps any assistance? Are you able to climb?" he bellowed out in a thick Cockney accent.

Ramses' men turned over weak and looked up

at the commander. They called up to the ship in almost a whisper.

"Yes, we can climb! Thank you, sir! You've saved us from certain death," the men responded cheerfully.

Commander Marlowe's head disappeared behind the bulwark of the ship for a moment. After only a few moments, his head reappeared over the rail again and two of his men rolled a rope ladder down to the men in the boat.

Ramses' men smiled slyly in anticipation, but still pretended to be too weak to grab the ladder. They began to slowly ascend up the ladder.

The first man on the ladder looked up at the bulwark as he climbed, but did not see the commander anymore. Both men pulled pistols from the back of their pants and cocked them just before they reached the top of the rail.

The first man jumped over the bulwark and screamed like a wild man, then, disappeared from the sight of his partner behind him on the rope ladder.

The second man on the ladder was confused. He heard none of the commotion that usually ensued after one or more of the pirates would successfully board an unsuspecting ship. He heard nothing from his partner but dead silence immediately after he jumped over the bulwark.

Finally, the second man on the ladder summoned all of his courage. He checked his pistol, then climbed the last few rungs of the ladder. Once at the top, he flung himself over the rail using his left hand and gripped his one shot pistol tightly in his right. The second pirate yelled loudly and pointed his pistol. When his feet hit the planks on the deck of the British vessel, he was shocked to find the first man over the rail with his hands raised to the sky and his pistol laying harmlessly on the deck to his right. Thirty of her Majesty's Marines, wearing their familiar red coats, had muskets trained on them. He gulped, then closed his eyes as he dropped his pistol to the deck and raised his hands slowly.

Commander Marlowe smirked smugly as he stood on the right side of the British Marines with a lace handkerchief in his left hand. His next command he delivered calm, cool and collected.

"Fire!"

The Marines discharged their weapons in unison. Fire shot out of the tips of their musket barrels.

Both of Ramses' men were riddled by discharged round balls and were blown backwards over the bulwark of the ship tumbling aimlessly back into the murky depths of the sea.

A lookout in the crow's nest at the top of the main mast saw Ramses' ship closing in on them from their stern side through his brass spyglass. He lowered the looking glass from his eye quickly and looked down at the commander. The lookout cupped his hands around his mouth and yelled down frantically.

"Commander! A ship approaches from stern side, sir! She's comin' in hard and fast, sir!"

Commander Marlowe ran to the stern of the ship. Quickly, he grabbed the spyglass from inside of his bright red coat, pulled it open and peered through it in the direction of Ramses' swift approaching vessel.

"That's it... come on. I have you now. That's it. Today you will die!" Commander Marlowe said to himself.

The commander collapsed his spyglass and

turned to his crew. He stood stiff at attention. About to pontificate, he placed his hands behind his back.

"Men, this is the day we've waited for! You and I have spent the better part of five years playing cat and mouse with this scum! I say that today be the day we regain our honor so that we can return to mother England with heads held high! Death to Ramses and his cutthroats!"

Commander Marlowe threw his right fist into the air. His entire crew followed suit and thrust their right fists into the air as well and decreed in unison.

"Death to Ramses!"

The commander glared at his men with pride and determination. He clicked his heels together and snapped to salute them before barking orders.

"For Queen and Country! To your battle stations!"

Three drummer boys began to beat the call to general quarters on their drums. Every crewmen and Royal Marine ran to their designated battle stations.

The drummer boy in the center of the other

two was a cute mulatto boy. His eyes were green and his hair was sun bleached and curly. The other two drummer boys that flanked him were Caucasian. The mulatto drummer boy turned his head into the direction of Commander Marlowe and scowled as he continued to play.

On the deck of his ship, the *Cimarron*, Ramses stood stoically on the bow as he looked through an ornate gold spyglass. His features had become more distinguished. His hair was medium-length dreadlocks and it blew in the wind. He wore a thick black full-length duster coat. The wind blew the coat back and revealed his custom shotgun pistols, which were held at his waist by custom crafted holsters. Under his arms were two pearl-handled one-shot pistols. Ramses lowered the spyglass from his eye and thought to himself.

Scars walked up behind Ramses.

"What's wrong?"

"We should have gotten the signal from those two by now. Something's wrong, I can feel it," said Ramses with concern.

Scars laughed hardily and slapped Ramses on the back.

"You worry too much, big fella. How long have we been doing this," asked Scars, unconvinced that there was anything to worry about.

Ramses lifted his spyglass to his eye again. Apprehensively he spoke to Scars once more.

"Too long, that's what worries me. Tell the men to be ready for anything on this one. Pass out some hand mortars and volley guns to some of the men, just in case."

"Will do... El Capitan!" Scars answered playfully, then turned and walked to the middle of the deck, as Ramses continued to peer through his spyglass. Behind him, Scars barked orders.

"Listen up! The big fella wants the boarding party to have hand mortars and volley guns, so let's get it done," he said and clapped his hands and shooed them away like children. Ramses' crewmen began to scurry about the deck with purpose.

Back aboard the *Badger*, Commander Marlowe kept his eyes trained on Ramses' frigate as it approached their position rapidly. Marlowe turned to his men, calm and confident.

"We must not lose the element of surprise,

Gentlemen! Everyone is to keep low to the deck until it is time for us to spring our trap!"

The British crewmen and Royal Marines began to take up hidden positions behind the bulwarks. Some also laid face down onto the deck itself. The adolescent drummers continued to beat out "General Quarters".

Commander Marlowe craned his head in the direction of the trio of drummers, aggravated.

"Will you quit that infernal racket," he chided.

All three of the boys were startled and stopped playing abruptly. Two of the drummers dropped their heads in fear of the commander. But, the mulatto boy did not.

He glared up at Commander Marlowe defiantly as he removed the drum strap from around his neck. The boy then lifted his drum over his small head and slammed the drum on the deck and broke it into pieces.

The commander became beside himself in anger. He stared at the mulatto boy for a brief moment, then, summoned his Leftenant who was standing near the drummers.

"Take that one below and teach him to honor

the Queen's uniform and equipment," he ordered angrily, as he pointed at the mulatto drummer boy.

The Leftenant spun quickly and grabbed the defiant little drummer under his right arm. Forcefully, he was taken below deck.

The mulatto boy clutched one of his drumsticks in his left hand. He resisted as much as he could before being taken through the doors that led to the bowels of the ship.

Below deck, the Leftenant became increasingly frustrated with the struggling boy down the creaky wooden steps. The officer stopped in the middle of the stairs and backhanded the boy in the face to force him to comply. He raised his pointer finger into the mulatto boy's face and chastised him in a thick British accent.

"If you continue this behavior, I swear to Christ Almighty, I'll slap all of the black off that little body of yours! Am I makin' meself clear enough for ya?"

The mulatto boy stopped his complaining and cursing immediately as he scowled at the Leftenant.

"Monsieur, I will kill you for striking me! Am I making myself clear?"

The mulatto drummer decreed in French before intentionally spitting blood onto the white British uniform pants and socks of the officer. He lifted his head and smiled at the Leftenant with bloodstained teeth.

The Leftenant infuriated, lifted his right hand above his head to strike the lad. But, he quickly regained his composure and slowly lowered his hand. The officer instead, grabbed the drummer, picked him up and threw him over his right shoulder and started down the creaky steps once more.

The mulatto drummer still clutched one of his drumsticks in his right hand. Suddenly, he jabbed the tip of it into a crack between the boards in the hull of the ship and broke it off, which left a jagged point. Then without hesitation began to jab the broken drumstick into the neck of the Leftenant with reckless abandon.

The stunned officer threw the boy down the remaining steps and grabbed for the wounds in his neck with his right hand as he pulled a handkerchief from inside his red coat simultaneously with his left. As fast as he could, the Leftenant tied it tightly around his neck so that the bleeding punctures were covered.

The small drummer tumbled down the remaining steps. Once at the bottom, he rolled over and jumped to his feet but immediately fell back to the floor when a sharp pain shot up his leg because of a badly sprained ankle he'd acquired from his fall down the stairs. The boy took a quick glance down a narrow corridor.

To either side of the corridor were thick wooden doors designed to keep people in. The boy turned and looked up the steps and saw the Leftenant stumbling down them toward him. The wounded officer applied pressure to the wounds in his neck with his right hand and pulled his saber from his right hip with his left. Furious, the Leftenant pointed it angrily at the mulatto boy.

The injured boy crawled away as fast as he could toward the narrow corridor on his hands and knees.

The Leftenant struggled to catch the boy. He swiped at him with his saber, but missed and hit the wall.

The little drummer crawled to the end of the

corridor, then realized he had nowhere else to escape to. The brave little drummer turned to face his fate. The Leftenant smiled as he raised his saber over his head.

The mulatto boy summoned all the strength he had left inside of his tiny body and lifted himself off the floor high enough to slide the wooden latch to the cell door next to him open, then fell helplessly to the floor again.

The Leftenant seized the opportunity and brought his saber down to strike the boy a final blow.

Without warning, the cell door the boy had unlatched swung open violently and jolted the Leftenant, knocking him into the wall opposite the cell.

His eyes widened as a hulking, bald, dark skinned man stood in the door of the cell with not much room in the doorway to either side of him. The officer swung his saber up at the gigantic bald man.

The huge released prisoner grabbed the right wrist of the Leftenant and broke the saber in half with his foot against the wall. Then grabbed the petrified officer by the throat and twisted. The mulatto boy smirked as he could hear the bones in the Leftenant's neck breaking.

The hulking bald man continued to twist the Leftenant's head around until it faced in the opposite direction. He released the dead officer and allowed his body to tumble limply to the dank floor. The man turned and looked down at the boy— who was still wearing an intense scowl upon his face— then smiled as he bent down and picked the mulatto boy up gently from the floor and hugged him affectionately.

The boy smiled widely and closed his eyes as he held the gigantic bald man's neck. He lifted his head and looked into the eyes of the bald man.

"It is good to see you, Toussaint! I thought I would never see you again!"

Toussaint smiled, then replied. "Nor I you, little master Guy! But where is your sister? We must find her and leave this ship immediately!"

Guy scanned the doors of the brig.

"She should be down here as well. Monique! Monique!" he cried out desperately, then listened as hard as he could for Monique's voice.

Guy and Toussaint were relieved when they

heard the muffled voice of a little girl coming from the first door at the beginning of the corridor.

"Je suis ici! Je suis ici!" [I am in here! I am in here!] Monique cried out frantically.

Toussaint without hesitation swept Guy up in his arms and ran towards the sound of Monique's voice.

Up top on the deck of the British vessel *Badger*, Commander Marlowe pulled his saber from its scabbard and kissed it ceremonially. He lowered himself behind the bulwark with his men and awaited Ramses' ship eagerly. To make sure they would not lose the element of surprise, Marlowe turned to his men and motioned with his hand for them to stay low.

Both ships were in close proximity to each other now. Ramses' ship pulled alongside the *Badger* silently. But the deck of the *Cimarron* seemed empty and silent as well.

The Royal Marine officer knelt behind the bulwark next to his men. He lifted his one shot pistol and slowly cocked the hammer back as quietly as he could. One of his men, a young Marine, shook nervously beside the officer. He looked up at his commander, sweating profusely, with paralyzing fear frozen upon his face. The Marine officer smiled at the young Marine and patted him on the shoulder to steady him. The young Marine held his musket tighter in his hands and took a deep calming breath. He looked up, nodded his head and smiled at the Marine officer.

Suddenly, a bell pepper sized grenade dropped to the deck behind them. Both men turned and saw it. The grenade rolled between the two of them with the fuse sizzling.

The Marine officer pushed the young Royal Marine away from the grenade as it ignited, but to no avail. The grenade blew both men through the rail, killing them instantly.

The rail they were hiding behind blew apart. Commander Marlowe jumped to his feet and saw the gaping hole in the bulwark made by the grenade. He hurried to the center of the deck and raised his saber.

"Fire at will! Fire at will!" he ordered with confidence.

The red coated Royal Marines stood simultaneously with muskets raised and prepared to fire on Ramses' vessel, but were confused when they had nothing to target. They swayed their muskets to the right, then to the left as they searched desperately for a viable target.

After a few tense moments, the Royal Marines could not believe their eyes as they saw ten arms from behind the bulwark of the *Cimarron* lob lit grenades towards them.

The Marines watched the grenades in flight over their heads, then scrambled in different directions. The grenades hit the deck of the *Badger* and exploded almost simultaneously. The section of the ship that the Royal Marines were positioned in erupted into a ball of fire.

Instantly, men aboard the British vessel screamed and cried out in agony. Some were on fire and leapt from the ship to extinguish themselves in the sea. Others were burned beyond recognition on deck. A British crewman lay in a pool of blood with nails and splinters from the ship lodged in his face and body. A Royal Marine crawled away from the blast area on his elbows. His legs had been blown off below his knees.

Merely 20 feet away from the chaos caused

by the grenade attack, Royal Marines and British crewmen still cowered by the rail facing the *Cimarron*.

Six pirates stood suddenly on the deck of the pirate vessel. Each of them pointed hand mortars toward the British crewman and Marines hiding behind the bulwark. They fired the mortars at their target. Three Royal Marines fired their muskets from the crow's nest on the main mast of the *Badger* and hit their mark. Three pirates that hid behind the bulwark of the *Cimarron* clutched their faces, yelled and fell to the deck.

Scars saw three of his men fall. He looked up at the Royal Marine sharpshooters, perched in the crow's nest, reloading their muskets. Bravely, he stood from behind the rail and brought the hand mortar up, took aim and with a loud boom fired the weapon at the sharpshooters. The nest exploded into incendiary pieces. The sharpshooters manning their post were blown into oblivion.

Two more British crewmen were hit upon the head and concussed as yet another projectile from a hand mortar ignited when it crashed into the bulwark of the *Badger* and exploded instantly.

Four Royal Marines stood and fired their muskets at the men on the *Cimarron*.

Two pirates holding mortars were hit by the Marine's volley and they fell to the deck in different contorted positions. Two of the remaining pirate mortar crew fired a deafening volley towards the *Badger*, then took cover behind the rail of the *Cimarron*.

When their rounds of mortars exploded on the deck of the heavily damaged British vessel, Commander Marlowe was blown into the large ship's wheel by the shockwave created by them. Screams of immense pain ensued after the blast as many of the remaining Royal Marines were blown over the side of the ship.

Commander Marlowe shook his head as he attempted to regain focus. He felt for, and then grabbed one of the spindles in the center of the wheel to pull himself to his feet. His eyes refocused and he scanned the deck to assess the status of his men in the fierce battle. The Commander heroically unsheathed his saber and lifted it into the air so that his remaining men could see him.

"Rally on me! Rally on me, men! Prepare to repel boarders! Form a skirmish line here," he commanded in a voice filled with determination, as he lowered his saber and carved a line in the wood of the deck to show his remaining men where he wanted the line. A few wounded crewmen and ten Marines rallied to the commander's position at the helm with muskets in hand.

On the deck of the *Cimarron*, Ramses and his men rose simultaneously from behind the cover of their ship's rail, shouting war cries! Ramses was holding one of his custom shotgun pistols in his left hand and a cutlass in his right. His men were armed with boarding axes, cutlasses and belaying pins.

Scars and four other pirates arose from behind the bulwark, as well, twirling grappling hooks over their heads. The sound of the grappling hooks cutting through the wind could be heard as they twirled. Scars smirked sinisterly before he gave the order to his men.

"Now!"

He and his four men released the hooks at the same time. Each of the grappling hooks hit their mark. Then they all rapidly pulled the slack from their ropes. Scars and the others quickly tied the ropes around cleats located on the bulwark of the *Cimarron* to secure both vessels to one another. Ramses and his crew backed away from the bulwark slowly. He nodded to Scars. Scars nodded back. They both turned and looked over at the burning deck of the *Badger*. Through the smoke, they saw Commander Marlowe and the rest of his men with muskets and pikes trained at them.

Ramses war cried then ran toward the *Badger* ahead of his men. Scars and the rest of the pirate crew followed closely behind Ramses, as they yelled and began to attack.

Commander Marlowe watched as Ramses and his men leapt over his bulwark. The brave commander raised his saber with purpose. He pointed his weapon in the direction of the oncoming invaders of his vessel and gave a desperate order.

"Fire!" he yelled at the top of his lungs.

Ramses, Scars, and their men were in midair, in the space between the two mammoth ships. Musket balls ripped through many of Ramses' men while in the air. Two pirates were hit and the force repelled them back over the bulwark of the *Badger* and into the sea. Scars grabbed the side of his face and fell to the deck of the *Badger* motionless. Five more pirates clutched their faces and stomachs when the British round balls ripped through them.

Commander Marlowe looked on with disdain as Ramses and the rest of his screaming pirates dropped onto the deck of his ship. He skillfully thrust the tip of his saber into an attacking pirate's throat that ran at him with cutlass in hand. Then, he picked up a one shot pistol that was lying next to a dead Royal Marine who had been shot between the eyes. The commander made the sign of the cross over the Marine, then stood erect once more.

"Men... with me! With me," he yelled stoically.

When Ramses landed on the deck of the *Badger*, he rolled athletically and jumped to his feet. Two British crewmen attempted to stab him with pikes. He blocked the pike thrusts of the crewman to his right with his cutlass and slashed him across the front of his torso leaving a horribly deep gash in him. Simultaneously, he blasted the crewman to his left with his custom shotgun pistol, in the stomach, knocking him backward off his feet.

Commander Marlowe aimed the pistol at Ramses. He squinted as he tried to get a clear shot through the thick smoke from the fires on deck. He was unable to get a clear shot which frustrated him.

Ramses blocked the bayonet of a Royal Marine and hacked him down with the cutlass. He then ran, jumped and kicked an attacking British crewman in the face and knocked him to the deck. He stabbed the man in the stomach as he yelled wildly.

Just as Ramses looked up and saw Commander Marlowe and smiled, a Royal Marine attempted to attack Ramses from behind with his saber above his head, poised to strike. At that moment, a musket blast rang out. Ramses ducked and turned in time to see the Royal Marine drop his saber and clutch his own throat, before he fell to the deck coughing up blood.

Ramses squinted through the smoke in the direction that the timely musket shot came from.

He smiled slyly and nodded when he saw Scars lying on the deck with an aimed musket with smoke still seeping from its barrel. He turned quickly, only to find Commander Marlowe holding the pistol in his face.

The commander smirked smugly at Ramses.

Ramses raised his hands in the air slowly and smirked, "Tell your men to drop their weapons!"

Ramses looked around at the ongoing battle for the ship, then brought his attention back to the commander.

"Now commander...why would I want to do that?" he responded calmly.

Commander Marlowe cocked the hammer back on the pistol.

"Because, if you do not, I will be forced to paint my deck with the contents of your miserable skull," he rebutted just as calmly as Ramses.

Ramses thought about the commander's ultimatum for a moment, then glanced over Commander Marlowe's left shoulder. He smirked at the commander and laid his cutlass and shotgun pistol onto the deck. Ramses turned and saw his pirates finishing off the remnants of

Commander Marlowe's men. Confident, he turned back to Marlowe.

"Commander, if I were you... I'd think of surrendering your weapon. You have lost. There is no honor in dying for a lost cause. Now surrender, before I become angry with you." Ramses replied in a serious tone.

Commander Marlowe was furious and unrelenting.

"I may die, but at least I'll die with the satisfaction of ridding the sea of you and your floating zoo!" Commander Marlowe smiled, as he was ready to discharge his weapon into Ramses' face.

Suddenly, a massive black hand grabbed Commander Marlowe around the neck from behind and began to choke the life from him. The commander's eyes widened and bulged as he gurgled from the intense pressure being applied to his windpipe. The one shot pistol he held fell harmlessly to the deck. Ramses, Scars, and the rest of their remaining men all laughed hysterically.

Commander Marlowe was lifted off his feet and turned around to see that he was in the unbreakable grip of Toussaint. Toussaint choked Marlowe with both hands, as Guy and Monique stood on opposite sides of him. Toussaint continued to choke the commander as he spoke to him.

"Je vous aid it que j'allais obstruer la merde hors de vous, si je sortais jamais, vous morceau anlais de merde!" [I told you I was going to choke the shit out of you if I ever got out, you English piece of shit!]

Guy yanked at the bottom of Toussaint's shirt.

"Toussaint, assez!" [Enough!]

Toussaint released his grip on Commander Marlowe's neck and threw him to the deck like a rag doll. He walked toward the commander to grab him again.

Without warning, cannon fire from an unseen vessel erupted. Toussaint stopped walking towards the commander. He quickly swept up Guy and Monique into his powerful arms and covered them with his thick body.

Commander Marlowe gasped for oxygen. He struggled, but rolled over, got to his feet and dove overboard into the ocean.

Almost at the same time a cannonball hit the starboard side of the *Badger* and blew a massive hole in her. Scars ran to the starboard bulwark of the ship. He strained his eyes to see the origin of ship that was firing upon them and approaching their position rapidly.

The oncoming vessel was cutting through the sea fast and was flying the familiar British flag on its stern. The attacking British ship fired from its two cannons, positioned at its bow. The two cannonballs whistled through the air over the smoky *Badger*.

Scars turned to the crew in a panic.

"Ramses, it is a British War Frigate...and she's coming for us!"

Ramses picked up his shotgun pistol and cutlass off the deck, then, turned to his men with a new sense of urgency.

"It's a goddamn trap! Everyone back to the *Cimarron*! We will take them to the caye!"

Ramses' men began to quickly vacate the *Badger* and jumped back to the *Cimarron*. A cannonball hit the stern of the *Badger* and sent debris and fire into the air. A second missed and plunged into the sea.

Ramses backed up to get a running start to jump to his ship. Before he leapt, he glanced over at Toussaint and saw him still protecting the children with his own body.

"Ahoy, large one!"

Toussaint turned his head in Ramses' direction.

"I cannot offer you any other kind of life but that of we pirates! I owe you my life, and to a Mandinka, this means I can't let you die until that debt is fulfilled, or I shall live in torment in the afterworld!"

Toussaint nodded to Ramses. He stood and held Guy and Monique's tiny hands in his. Ramses smirked at Toussaint, then ran and leaped to the deck of the *Cimarron*. He again rolled over athletically, stood, and turned. Ramses signaled to Toussaint and held his arms out to the exceptionally large man.

Toussaint looked down at Monique. He grabbed her by the back of her shirt and leg, then lifted her up and tossed her over to the awaiting Ramses with ease. Toussaint repeated the same motion and threw the protesting young Guy over the rail to the *Cimarron* into the awaiting arms of Ramses.

After successfully tossing the children to safety, Toussaint prepared to leap to the *Cimarron* as well. He backed away from the rail until his back bumped into the opposite bulwark. Toussaint took in a deep breath before running as fast as he could toward the *Cimarron*. Just before he reached the bulwark, the huge man jumped awkwardly through the air. It appeared that he wouldn't make it all the way across the expanse from ship to ship, but he did land safely onto the deck of the *Cimarron*.

The rapidly approaching British ship fired another volley from its bow cannon as he touched down on deck. The projectiles hit the *Badger* and exploded violently behind Toussaint. The heavily damaged vessel began to sink, as the entire ship became engulfed in flames.

Guy and Monique ran over to Toussaint and lifted their arms to him. He bent over and picked both of them up, relieved they were not injured during the transfer from the *Badger*.

Ramses nodded to Toussaint.

"Welcome aboard the *Cimarron*! She is not much to look at, but she is paid for! It will be safer for the children below deck, my large friend!" Ramses shouted to the new arrivals as his men scurried to their battle stations.

Guy, hearing Ramses' suggestion scowled at him. "I am not a child, sir! I can help you fight the English!" Guy yelled at Ramses in English with an angry French accent.

Ramses smiled and patted Guy on the head with his left hand. He knelt down in front of Guy and looked him in the eyes.

"I know you are not a child, young warrior. But I need you to follow orders without question and get below deck to protect your sister, do you understand?"

Guy pondered for a moment. He looked at Monique, then back at Ramses. The boy snapped to attention like a tiny soldier and saluted Ramses with his right hand, then turned his head slightly towards Toussaint.

"Oui, Monsieur! Toussaint, we will take Monique below deck for her protection!"

Ramses returned a salute to Guy in token seriousness. "You may carry on!"

Toussaint looked at Ramses with appreciation.

Ramses became serious again. He ran to the starboard side of his ship and pulled the spyglass from inside his black coat. The pirate captain spread it open and held it up to his right eye and saw the British frigate with three rows of cannons exposed out the side of the ship.

The frigate fired the bow cannon once again sending deadly chunks of iron whistling through the air. Fortunately for the crew of the *Cimarron*, they both splashed harmlessly into the sea in front of the pirate ship.

Ramses collapsed his spyglass and ran to the bow of the ship. He turned to his men.

"They are trying to block our access to the inlet! Prepare for a high-speed broadside! Set a collision course!"

Ramses yelled an order to a short and scrawny crewman, with unkempt blonde hair and appeared malnourished, "Spider Monkey, let fly the colors!"

Scars was at the helm of the ship. He spun the wheel to the left frantically. The wind filled the sails of the *Cimarron* once again and it turned tightly away from the doomed *Badger*. Scars spun the wheel back to the right and steered the

Cimarron into a collision course with the British warship.

Spider Monkey went into action immediately and began to climb the rope ladder to the top of the main mast in the center of the *Cimarron* deck. Once he reached the top, the agile crewman removed the long black leather cover off the ship's flag.

The flag was massive and unfurled as the wind caught it. It was black, handsewn and about the size of a king sized bed sheet. In the center were the familiar skull and crossbones, but through the top of the skull was a pirate's cutlass with an Egyptian ankh on the cutlass' handle. Finally, the skull's mouth was open as if it were screaming into a stiff wind. Their unique Jolly Roger fluttered violently in the wind.

Ramses made his way to the bow of the *Cimarron* and peered through his spyglass once more.

"Batteries... at the ready," he commanded in a military manner.

Scars repeated his command loudly.

"All batteries, at the ready!"

Immediately, square wooden covers were

removed from below deck that revealed hidden cannon turrets cut into the hull of the *Cimarron*. The muzzles of multiple cannons were simultaneously pushed into firing position. The last covers removed were directly below where the pirate captain was standing. Then, two huge cannon muzzles were pushed into view from those openings. Ramses looked down at the large black iron muzzles and smiled sinisterly, before he lifted his spyglass to his right eye again.

"All right, boys! It's time to let them know whose piece of ocean they now have the misfortune of sailing in! Bow cannon only... Fire!"

Scars repeated Ramses order loudly, with a hyper-intense expression on his sweaty face.

"Bow guns only-- Fire!"

The two huge guns erupted and spit fire. Ramses raised the spyglass to his eye to assess the gun's aim. Through his spyglass he witnessed one of the cannonballs fall short of the oncoming British frigate. But the second was a direct hit and ripped through the frigate's main sail.

Ramses smirked as he lowered the spyglass

and turned his head slightly to the right toward Scars.

"You're right on 'em, boys! Two degrees lower, then give those red-coated bastards hell!"

Scars screamed Ramses' order as he watched the main mast of the British vessel coming directly for the *Cimarron*.

"Bow guns only! Two degrees lower! And you better blow these limey sons-of-bitches out of our way!"

Ramses stood stoically on the bow of the *Cimarron* as the two ships sailed toward one another on a collision course at a high rate of speed. He glanced into the sunny skies above and closed his eyes. The spyglass he dropped to the deck and opened his arms as wide as they would spread.

"Oh great Nyame, hear me now! I accept whatever fate you deem fit. I ask only this for my sacrifice... freedom and long life for my beloved Fulani. Watch over her and keep her safe wherever she may be! Do this and I shall be your warrior on the other side. Do this not and I will make war on you in the afterlife! To this I swear!"

The British warship fired its bow guns once again. One of the cannonballs hit the ocean at the base of the *Cimarron's* hull in front of where Ramses was saying his prayer. Water sprayed him. The other projectile struck the *Cimarron's* figurehead, a carving of a beautiful woman whose hair looked as if it were blowing in the wind, was left of Ramses. It not only damaged the figurehead's body, but ripped through the bow rail as well.

Scars dove to the deck, then looked up at the defiant Ramses still on the bow of the ship. Scars' expression turned to one of confusion as his friend stood there unprotected, with his arms stretched out. It was as if Ramses wanted to be struck down by a British cannonball.

Ramses opened his eyes once more and yelled at the top of his lungs, "Fire!"

The two cannons below him spat fire once again. Ramses looked up and smiled into the sky when he saw the thick wooden main mast of the British warship splintered by a direct cannonball hit and fall to the deck.

All of Ramses' men cheered as they watched the most important piece of equipment on the attacking ship explode and tumble downward. Ramses smirked, then turned and ran over to Scars who was still looking at him quizzically and concerned.

"Are you alright, big fella? Because you are really starting to worry me!"

Ramses looked at him and smiled reassuringly. "I'm doing better than those red coats over there are going to be. Now, I want you to keep this heading, no matter what, do you understand? Are you up for this?" Ramses asked with some concern about Scars' ability to carry his strategy out.

Scars seemed unsure. He took a deep breath and shook his body and tried to loosen himself up. Taking in another deep breath, he closed his eyes to calm himself. He opened them again and his facial expression went from intense concern to a slowly, widening smile.

"I would follow you into hell with kerosene underbritches, my friend."

Ramses smiled proudly and placed his hand on his friend's shoulder. He then turned with urgency to his men on deck.

"Men, we are going to ram the *Cimarron* up

their royal ass! I want volley gun crews on the larboard bulwark," he shouted to the crew on deck. Then he turned his attention to the cannon crew.

"Cannon Crews?"

Below, the pirate cannon crews hung on every word from their captain as they manned their individual cannons.

"Aye, Captain," they responded collectively.

"We are going to head straight for this frigate until the last possible moment. I need you all to pour as much iron into their hull as you can! Are you with me?"

The entire crew pumped their fists angrily into the air, all primed for a fight. They loved their captain and were willing to die for him.

"Ramses! Ramses! Ramses!" the pirate crew chanted in unison.

Ramses ran to the bow of the *Cimarron* again. He saw the British frigate fire another volley from its bow guns. The pirate vessel was moving so fast through the water that the cannonballs sailed harmlessly into its wake.

The two vessels were in very close proximity to one another when Ramses turned his head back to Scars and raised his left hand into the air. Again, Ramses turned his attention back to the warship. Ten pirates ran to the larboard bulwark as instructed and stood at the ready, as they aimed their volley guns.

"More speed! More speed! Now Scars, now!" Ramses ordered frantically.

Scars jumped quickly from behind the wheel and pushed a long wooden lever next to the main mast of the ship. Afterwards, a collection of pulleys and gears went into motion inside the belly of the *Cimarron*.

Suddenly, two horizontal mast sections dropped into place, attached to the existing mast, and revealed two more large sections of sail for three times the available wind collection. The sails filled with air instantly.

Ramses, Scars, and the men all grabbed hold of whatever they could to keep from falling as the ship lurched into more knots abruptly and went much faster than before. More of the ship's bow raised out of the sea as it picked up speed from the updrafts that filled the new sections of sail.

Toussaint and the children were thrown to the

floor of the cabin as the ship shifted into a higher speed.

The British frigate fired its bow guns. The *Cimarron* too, fired upon the British vessel with its bow guns. Both ships sustained major damage from the direct hits that ensued.

The captain of the British warship stood on the bow of his ship determined to bring Ramses' pirate band to justice. Ramses also continued to stand on the bow of the *Cimarron* defiantly.

The two ships were less than one thousand yards from each other on a collision course. The ships were so close that Ramses could see the British frigates' contingent of Royal Marines running into position on deck without the use of his spyglass.

Scars gripped the wheel tightly and sweated nervously. He kept his eyes trained on Ramses. Suddenly, Ramses turned and ran to the larboard bulwark where he had the men with volley guns positioned. He pulled his shotgun pistols from their holsters and stood beside them at the ready.

"Scars... hard to starboard," he commanded.

Scars immediately spun the ship's wheel to the right as hard and as fast as he could.

The *Cimarron* turned hard and revealed much of her bottom. It appeared to be in danger of capsizing. Ramses and his men with volley guns fired at the British frigate as they passed.

The British captain was seen on deck with his saber in hand. He implored the Royal Marines to fire on the pirate ship. The Marines were in two lines on deck. The men in the first line knelt down.

Ramses fired his shotgun pistol at the British frigate. The ten pirates to Ramses' right fired their volley guns at the Marines. Several of the Royal Marines were hit and fell to the deck wounded or dead, four of them from the back line and three soldiers who knelt in front.

The British frigate fired all available cannons on the side the *Cimarron* passed them on. Explosions ripped through the hull of the *Cimarron*. Three of the *Cimarron's* cannon crews took direct hits and were knocked out of action. The remaining cannon crew of the *Cimarron* fired in succession. Each exposed barrel of the *Cimarron* spat fire as it passed the warship.

Both ships sustained heavy damage. The

Cimarron and the British frigate were both ablaze.

Scars looked back at the crippled British warship behind them excited.

"Goddamnit! I think I gotta change my drawers!"

Ramses stood and tried to assess the damage of his vessel quickly. He turned to Scars.

"Scars... you still here?" he asked jokingly.

Scars turned in Ramses' direction and gave him a smile and thumbs up.

"Head for the inlet," ordered Ramses.

He turned to the remainder of his crew.

"You men form some bucket crews and put these damn fires out!"

Ramses looked into the sky.

"Once again, you have not allowed me to join you, Mighty One. I humbly thank you again for saving my worthless hide."

Ramses walked to the stern of the *Cimarron* and watched as the British frigate burned and filled the sky with thick black smoke before descending to the deep.

CHAPTER 27

LETTER OF MARQUE

Ramses, Scars, Toussaint and the children walked down the gangplank to the dock of the pirate compound. Ramses' men picked the bodies of their dead off the deck of the *Cimarron* and carried them down to the sand where they piled them up.

Ramses looked up at the front gate of the compound as they approached it. He frowned his face in confusion.

"Where are all of the guards?" he asked Scars rhetorically.

Scars ran up to the main gate and swung it open. To his surprise, five Royal Marines cocked their musket hammers and pointed them in his face.

Ramses reached for his custom shotguns, but 30 more Royal Marines appeared on top of the main wall and trained their muskets down at him, Toussaint and the children.

Toussaint started toward the Marines. Ramses grabbed him by his left arm. Toussaint turned and gave him an evil look. Ramses shook his head at the hulking man, dropped his pistols to the ground and raised his hands into the air. Toussaint paused for a moment, then complied and raised his hands as well. The rest of Ramses' crew walked up from the inlet docks with their hands raised and disarmed. Ramses and the others looked around the British infested compound perplexed.

A tall middle-aged admiral appeared from behind the Royal Marines at the main gate. He wore a fancy red uniform with multiple gold medals and ribbons on the right breast. On his head was a long grey wig and a Napoleon-styled hat. The Admiral walked with a black cane, as if he was taking a stroll in the park. He walked past Scars and headed towards Ramses. The British officer stopped directly in front of Ramses and bowed stylishly, as if he were in the king's court.

"Mr. Ramses, I presume?" Admiral Abercrombee asked like a British Aristocrat.

Ramses looked around still unsure what was happening. He lowered his hands.

"Yes, I am Ramses. And to whom do I have the misfortune of addressing?" he fearlessly asked.

Admiral Abercrombee pulled a handkerchief from inside his coat pocket and placed it up to his mouth.

"When I was sent here initially... it was to rid this land of your kind of fuckery! But as fate would have it, it seems that fortune has smiled upon you and your men. Let me also say that after your performance in battle today, I am quite impressed with you and your men's skill. This makes my new directive a little easier for me to swallow."

Ramses looked confused at the Admiral.

"What the hell are you talking about, English? Just shoot or hang us and get it over with! We are pirates and we all know what that means if you are apprehended! All I ask is that you allow the children and their caretaker to live... for they are not members of my crew!" Ramses blurted out in anger.

Admiral Abercrombee laughed hysterically, then, regained his composure.

"That was exactly what I planned on doing,

the moment, and I mean the very moment I laid eyes on you or any other member of your wretched crew!"

Scars made the sign of the cross, clasped his hands tightly together, closed his eyes and prayed as hard as he could silently.

Admiral Abercrombee continued.

"But, through some unholy twist of fate, I have received an urgent dispatch from the British War Department ordering me to cease and desist with my plans of executing you!"

The admiral cleared mucus from his throat exaggeratedly, then spat on the ground.

"You all deserve as slow and as painful a death as is humanly possible after all the lives you have taken and property you have stolen and etcetera! But, instead of a much deserved and earned death, I am on direct orders from the Crown to offer you and your vessel a *Letter of Marque!*"

Ramses looked at the admiral more quizzically than before.

"Pardon my ignorance, Captain, but what the hell are you saying?"

Annoyed, Admiral Abercrombee quipped, "I

am an Admiral, sir. Not a Captain!"

"Apologies, but what exactly is this *Letter of Marque* you speak of?" Ramses asked, deeply intrigued if it meant what he thought it did for he and his men.

Admiral Abercrombee clapped his hands as an astute looking young male assistant ran through the front gate clumsily and nervously past the detachment of Royal Marines, who still held their muskets aimed at Ramses and his men.

The assistant nervously approached where the admiral and Ramses parlayed. Once there, he knelt down and placed a small red, wooden box onto the ground in front of him. He lifted the lid of the box and removed a piece of parchment paper with words written in script on it. Lastly, he removed the quill and small bottle of ink.

The assistant stood and handed the letter to Admiral Abercrombee, then snapped to attention with the quill in his left hand and bottle of ink in his right.

Admiral Abercrombee pontificated in an official and military fashion.

"Yesterday morning, the British government declared war on the empire of Spain! The

Province of Florida is the contested prize of this conflict! The situation has become one of 'the enemy of my enemy is my friend!' So, in layman's terms a *Letter of Marque* means that you will be allowed to keep your illegal enterprises going, as long as it is performed only on vessels from the empire of Spain! A *Letter of Marque* makes you no longer a murderous, bloodthirsty pirate! It gives you an honored position in the British Royal Navy, as one of Her Majesty's *Privateers*.

Ramses pondered for a moment. He placed his right hand to his chin and thought hard. He looked up at the Marines on the compound wall and at the main gates with muskets pointed at Scars. He smirked when he saw Scars still praying as hard as he could. Ramses dropped his hand down and walked calmly toward the Admiral, smiling.

Admiral Abercrombee clutched his cane and pulled the handle up slightly, revealing the gleaming blade hidden inside.

"So, this *Letter of Marque* is really like a British license to steal?" Ramses asked calm and cool.

The Admiral scoffed condescendingly. "Crude interpretation... but, correct nonetheless, sir. You will be sailing in the name of the British Empire. What say you, sir? Will you accept the Queen's letter?"

Ramses turned his head to the right and looked at Scars who had opened his eyes to hear his answer. He also scanned the compound and saw his men with their hands raised. The pirate captain turned back to the admiral and smirked. "You bet your pasty white ass we will!"

To Be Continued

Preview of Book IV:

MOTHER OF VENGENCE:

CHAPTER 1

Sodom and Gomorrah

The air on the Bishop Plantation that evening was more humid and thick then usual. The smell of well-cured tobacco wafted into the air and mingled with the smoke from the Chinese opium pipes, that were freely passed around by the expensively dressed Slaveocrats in attendance for their monthly dose of debauchery and fighting spectacle.

It was another gathering of the most wealthy and powerful men in the southern part of North America. The year: 1720. The men of this exclusive fraternity called their clandestine organization simply, *The Society*. The members of The Society descended upon a different member's plantation every month for their explicit brand of entertainment.

Each plantation brought with them their most prized possessions; their fighting slaves. Every man of The Society had scoured the world in search of the most skilled killers to fight for them in the pits, as did their fathers before them.

The members coveted nothing as much as a champion fighting slave because of the wealth and notoriety owning a champion brought to their individual houses within The Society.

It was a carnival like atmosphere on the sprawling grounds of the Bishop Plantation that night. The main house was located in the center of 1,000 acres of cultivated wilderness, which sat between fertile tobacco fields and row upon row of sugar cane.

The Bishop's crops stretched as far as the eye could see in any direction. The house, built by Bishop the elder's father over a century before, had two-story floor to ceiling small paned windows and towering Romanesque support columns jutting from the wrap around porch in front. Every architectural detail was produced by skillful artisans in Europe and shipped piece by piece to North America. The structure was a testament to the wealth they had accumulated on the backs of many a stolen people from every corner of the globe.

The family enjoyed a widely celebrated reputation as being the wealthiest in the Coastal Carolinas. It was also notoriously known as one of the most brutal Slaveocracies in existence. But, the reputation that Captain Bishop enjoyed most was his family's legacy of finding and training some of the most feared and skilled fighting slaves The Society had ever seen.

The dull clanking of metal striking metal echoed across the Bishop Plantation that night. One by one, luxurious carriages rolled up to the front of the main house pulled by well-groomed steeds. The gentlemen who exited the carriages were well dressed with top hats and frilly-sleeved shirts. Male slaves dressed in black tails and white wigs rushed over to each carriage as they made their way up the main dirt road to the house.

The members of The Society rushed inside the house without hesitation, as to not miss another moment. Once inside, they knew they had entered another world. A world that whatever pleasure a man sought, could be experienced at the Bishop Plantation, or any of the designated plantations on The Society's circuit.

Beautiful, scantily clad pleasure slaves of all shapes, sizes and genders pranced provocatively around the elegantly appointed room. A line of naked well endowed male slaves stood in a line in front of two members of the society. Both men gazed, scrutinized and marveled at the physiques of each of the slaves, slow and methodical.

One of the members; the most effeminate of the two, grabbed the thick, flaccid penis of the slave who had the longest of them all, and lead him away by his manhood. All three men made their way up the grand winding stairway to the second level and disappeared behind a door to one of the many available chambers to the left of the long corridor.

Across from them stood eight naked, voluptuous female slaves of all shades. They smiled provocatively at The Society members who walked by and gazed upon them, as they tried to decide which female to choose for their pleasure.

An older member groped at the breast of a tall female. He turned to his friend and laughed before turning back and licking her right nipple. The old man looked at her and smiled, then he took her by the hand and led her toward the stairs eagerly. His friend followed suit and grabbed the hand of the girl who stood next in line. He took her by the arm and pulled her with him toward the stairs quickly, as not to be left by his friend.

A beautiful female slave of mixed race with long, thick, flowing black hair poured wine from a silver pitcher into the eager, wide opened mouth of an obese member. His face was covered in red wine, as he laughed hardily, before kissing the slave girl passionately.

Members and pleasure slaves in a backroom were intertwined in an orgy involving ten or more people. It was impossible to tell where one naked body began and the other ended. Occasionally, one of the people involved in this carnal dance would take a quick reprieve to grab the Chinese Opium pipe and inhale its intoxicating smoke. Once reinvigorated, they'd return to the ritual more stimulated and lustful then before.

Music filled every corner of the room,

provided by a quartet of slave violinists, who were situated in the main room to the right side of the enormous fireplace. Each man was dressed in white wigs and black tails.

Over the mantel of the fireplace hung a life sized portrait of the man who built this empire of human misery, Captain Bishop's father, the late, Ebenezer Bishop; one of the first Europeans to bring slaves into North America.

Many of The Society members danced the night away with their favorite female slave dance partners. Each female dancing slave wore the latest in European fashion; complete with silk gloves and beehive wigs.

Captain Bishop stood at the top of the landing next to the grand staircase and scanned the goings on in the main ballroom. He studied the festivities, looking for any slave who was not doing the job they were designated for, or any Society member who was not enjoying whatever perversion they preferred.

The captain saw his designated society nights as his take on one of his favorite bible stories, Sodom and Gomorrah. The captain was tall, of strong build and handsome. His hair was almost completely grey. He never took part in any of the pleasures he provided for his fellow members. What the captain lived for and almost all he thought about were the fighting slaves. It was his addiction.

Beside him stood his only son. He was the splitting image of Captain Bishop when he was a young man. Bishop the younger was as handsome as his father at his age and had a steely look about him. He too was of strong build, tall and was every bit a Bishop, with a mean streak a mile wide. From the day he was born, he was groomed to take over the Bishop Empire... ~~~

BOOK III: THE PRIVATEER

CR

ABOUT THE AUTHOR

Lennox Nelson, a proud native of South Philadelphia and alumnus of Syracuse University. Nelson's vast experiences from his world travels have enriched his life with future stories to be told. Some of which come to life in the BLACK NANCY series. He is proud to have developed his own brand of storytelling, Histoventure, which tells the stories that we haven't heard with a mixture of history, adventure and fiction. Lennox and his wife, Beverly, reside in the Washington DC area.

Stay in formed with Lennox Nelson at www. Blacknancy.net, follow on twitter @LennoxNelson and connect with other fans on the open and closed groups at facebook.com/BlackNancyFanClub!

Made in the USA
Charleston, SC
10 January 2017